A Journ

MIDLIFE ~~*Crisis*~~
BREAKTHROUGH

*Moving Beyond Stigmas & Struggles to Unleash
Confident & Worthy Modern-Day Women*

ALA LADD

MAS Services
PUBLISHERS
Cicero, NY

Copyright Page

Copyright © 2021 by Ala Ladd

Midlife ~~Crisis~~ Breakthrough: A Journey to Whole-Self Health

All rights reserved. No part of this publication may be reproduced, distributed, or transmitted in any form or by any means, including photocopying, recording, or other electronic or mechanical methods, without the prior written permission of the publisher, except in the case of brief quotations embodied in critical reviews and certain other noncommercial uses permitted by copyright law.

Although the author and publisher have made every effort to ensure that the information in this book was correct at press time, the author and publisher do not assume and hereby disclaim any liability to any party for any loss, damage, or disruption caused by errors or omissions, whether such errors or omissions result from negligence, accident, or any other cause.

Adherence to all applicable laws and regulations, including international, federal, state, and local governing professional licensing, business practices, advertising, and all other aspects of doing business in the US, Canada, or any other jurisdiction is the sole responsibility of the reader and consumer.

Neither the author nor the publisher assumes any responsibility or liability whatsoever on behalf of the consumer or reader of this material. Any perceived slight of any individual or organization is purely unintentional.

The resources in this book are provided for informational purposes only and should not be used to replace the specialized training and professional judgment of a health care or mental health care professional.

Neither the author nor the publisher can be held responsible for the use of the information provided within this book. Please always consult a trained professional before making any decision regarding treatment of yourself or others.

Unless otherwise noted, Scripture is taken from the New Century Version (NCV), copyright © 2005 by Thomas Nelson, Inc. All rights reserved.

Library of Congress Control Number: 2021921631

Paperback ISBN: 978-1-956643-01-5

eBook ISBN: 978-1-956643-00-8

CONTENTS

Read This First   vii
Dedication   ix
Epigraph   xi
Introduction   xiii

SECTION 1

The Beginning   3

1. Balancing Bummers   9
2. Continuing Concerns   17

SECTION 2

Active Belief   31

3. Re-Awakening   39
4. Intentionality   57
5. Becoming   64

SECTION 3

Active Listening   73

6. Listening to Hear   77
7. Listening to Learn   86
8. Listening to Lean In   93

SECTION 4

Active Living   103

9. Continue with Confidence   105
10. Continue With Balance   116
11. Whole-Self Health   121

   Final words   127
   You Can Help   131
   Acknowledgments   133
   About the Author   135
   References   137
   Speaking Topics   139
   End Notes   141

READ THIS FIRST

As a thank you for reading my inspiring journey, *Midlife* ~~*Crisis*~~ *Breakthrough*, I'd like to offer you a FREE Gift.

Midlife is challenging, but instead fixating on problems, this free eBook will share with you the unique benefits open to you during this important season of change and opportunity.

To get your free copy of:
10 Reasons Why Midlife is Marvelous
go to:
https://10reasons.gr8.com/

DEDICATION

This book is dedicated to my spouse who continues to be my #1 supporter. He encouraged me to obtain a master's degree to educate myself to be a better coach and leader for women. He never ceases to amaze me. We've withstood some fierce storms in our almost 30 years together, and I am thankful we are still united as we further our journeys to encourage others to wellness, balance, and living authentic lives of worship. Thank you, sweetheart.

#thankful, #blessed, #allglorytoGod

EPIGRAPH

Finding better life balance is accomplished by getting a better handle on the components of your life so that your heart and your mind are not pulled too far in any direction.

— Ala Ladd

INTRODUCTION

Crisis came too early for me. Society communicated that *midlife* for a woman was being on the "wrong side of forty." So why was I dealing with midlife related issues? I was far too young to find myself in the middle of a menopausal nightmare, to which there seemed no hope of awakening. I was not prepared for the changes; and the stigmas that came with *midlife* seemed to intensify the unfavorableness of this natural stage. Did I just say natural? Yes, *midlife* is a natural development in the life of a mature woman, which is often covered in a shroud of negativity.

It is true, midlife comes with many different challenges including hot flashes, night sweats, sleep problems, vaginal dryness, mood changes, slower metabolism, and weight gain. These represent some of

INTRODUCTION

the internal challenges that come with menopause. Sadly, there are stigmas associated with this transition that creates additional and often unnecessary external and environmental challenges as well. Dealing with internal body change compounded by external forces is exhausting and contributes to significant mental, physical, and social struggle.

Midlife for me, was a time of great loneliness which exacerbated an unfulfilled, intense desire to "belong." If only someone had taken the time to communicate a strategy to stabilize or even diminish these internal struggles and external conflicts, they might have saved me a great deal of heartache and helped me find greater joy through difficulty. I did not find that "someone," so I am determined to be that person for others. Therefore I decided to publish a trilogy of books to help women walk through menopause and beyond.

This is the first book of the trilogy. It is my personal story. In the first section, I reflect on my beginnings to share how my family and community impacted my formation in both positive and negative ways. The second section leaps to early midlife and shares how dismay transforms in a season of self-discovery. My search to belong sent me on a crusade to re-discover my meaning, purpose, and worth in this world. I began activating my belief and began seeking to become a better version of myself. With a new desire and calling to lead women to their full potential, I needed to find mine. This important section, will begin to walk through the Five D's: Determine, Discover, Dream, Decide, and Do.

The third section flows out of the second, which expounds on the importance of activating listening skills. Listening is an important key which prompts the journey of finding a better life balance. In the last section I talk about living in balance, and you will read how crisis no longer defines me, and why midlife became a season of breakthrough.

As you continue reading, I hope to inspire you to accept your past experiences so you too can find courage in crisis and confidence through conflict. May you be motivated to move forward with your life and be empowered to make a difference in your world. May reading my journey be an inspiration to yours.

SECTION 1

The Beginning

THE BEGINNING

When is the last time you reflected on the beginning of your life?

Childhood consists of formidable years that teach you how to behave, how to respond to situations, and mold you into the human you are today.

It is important that I start my story from the beginning because my experiences and outside influences are what formed me into the person I am. The family dynamic of my youth influenced this older me. Here is an example. I remember as a teen saying to myself, "I am not going to be like my mother." Well, my communication skills, mannerisms, reactions to situations, my gift of entertaining, and event organization skills are traits that were directly gleaned from my mom.

Regardless of my youthful ambition, I have grown into a woman who is very much like her mother. My family experiences and cultural influences, good and bad, have molded me into me.

Just the other day I was helping my son move out of his apartment and watched his cleaning habits imitate tips and tricks he learned from watching me. He might not even be aware of his actions, but I can often listen to my boys and see basic living skills that were gleaned from either my husband or myself.

*Our environment, our community,
and our culture molds us.*

Growing up in a family of eight with five siblings close in age, my upbringing can be described as a daily adventure. Adventure = "never a dull moment" and "always be on your toes." We grew up at what I endearingly call "the compound" located at the end of a peninsula surrounded by water and family. Our property on the beautiful lake, was a bit of paradise that took a *lot* of hard work to maintain. My father was fixated on teaching his children to be hard workers. I remember being five years old and carrying wood, raking leaves, picking up sticks, and removing pieces of cinderblock from dump truck sized loads of gravel. Hearing the roar of a chainsaw today still instantaneously takes me back to my childhood labor memories.

My father taught us a good work ethic, my mom ran an impeccable household, and we six kids spent a lot of time together. As I shared, living on "the compound" we were surrounded by family—which included my aunt, uncle, cousins, and in the summer my grandma and grandpa. Grandpa was my favorite as a young lady. I adored him and would follow him around everywhere. Grandpa was a businessman who cared for his family and took the lead on teaching the importance of hard work. So much of my character and skills today were gleaned from him, beginning at a very young age. Bartering, cost analysis, bulk purchasing, making homemade foods, and cooking for the masses are talents and abilities that I attribute to my short years of exposure to my grandpa.

My environment and experiences shaped me into me.

Having the privilege of growing up in a remote and sheltered environment, you might be wondering, what did we do when we were allowed off "the compound?" We spent time at church, attended a Christian school, and worked at our family business. I was privileged to grow up in a conservative Christian environment where I was grounded in solid biblical theology. Now maybe you picked up my book to read and you don't consider yourself a "spiritual" person. That is ok. This book is not an attempt to convert you or intimidate you. Spirituality is part of *my* story—my journey to finding my identity, my purpose, my value, worth, and experience better life balance and whole-self health.

Soon, I promise to dig in deeper, but I need to stay "in the beginning" for just a short bit.

Yes, I had the privilege of being taught what I like to call my "young theology." My life changed at the age of five years old at a kid summer club where someone was talking about Jesus, whom I had already learned about at church. This leader talked about hell and how Jesus died on the cross and rose again because he loves *me*. So, I listened to the message, believed, and asked God to help take away my sins and make me new.[1] I can remember to this day feeling the Holy Spirit come into my life. Instantly I felt this invisible bubble around me protecting from negative influences.

My theology grew from that day, and I continued to be taught many things about God and the Bible. I learned that God was living *in my heart* and that anyone, including me, who trusted in God would never be disappointed.[2] I was given tools and tips to live my life but still experienced trouble, hardships, disappoint-

SECTION 1

ment, burn out, and often felt like a failure in my walk with God. This "young theology" had taught me to do what others told me to do. I was told to "follow the rules" and "appear" good to others. I was taught to respect and obey my elders. Elders referred all adults that were older than me. I learned how to focus my attention on pleasing others, which is why I failed to experience this true life, joy, and peace that the Bible promised those who believe. My identity was given to me, and my life was out of balance.

Have you ever felt like your life is out of balance?

Do you still feel that way?

Keep with me and I will share how my life has turned around and how these experiences have made me into the amazing, confident woman I am today.

7

Chapter One
BALANCING BUMMERS

What do you visualize when you think of the word "balance?"

Some of you might picture a mom holding a baby, stirring dinner, talking on the phone, and wondering who is going to answer the doorbell that just rang. Maybe for you it is juggling work expectations, family responsibilities, social relationships, and the list goes on. We will dive deeper into the subject of balance a little further in this book, but it was in tenth grade that I first realized my life needed better balance.

My life came to a halt as a sophomore in high school when a challenge was given regarding the aim of my life during a weekly chapel service.

I was asked:

"What is your life focus?"

"What are your intentions with God?"

"How do your actions stack up?"

These were big questions I was unsure how to answer which was deeply distressing—so I began to cry. Deep heaving sobs erupted and my tears wouldn't stop.

In high school I was one active girl. I participated in sports like soccer, volleyball, track and field and I sang in a traveling girls' ensemble. I basically tried to be part of *any* social gathering I could. I was whole heartedly searching for a place to belong.

I was one lonely girl who was happy on the outside but broken to pieces within.

A born people pleaser, I often focused on helping others and dealt with negative experiences by "stuffing them" deep down inside. As a young lady, I did not know how to handle life's messy situations. Since I was taught to always keep a good appearance, I learned to tuck away the abuse and trauma that came my way.

Looking back, "tucked away" might be a bit too ambiguous. It might be better defined as "buried." I buried my mental, sexual, and emotional abuse so deep that when asked to give my personal testimony, I believed that my story was boring.

Accepting Jesus as my Lord and Savior at the age of five, I strove to be a "good girl" by staying away from drugs, alcohol, smoking, and sex. I did not use the words "perfect girl." As a middle child and a bit hyper, I always had a zest for life. If allowed, I would be found happily singing through my day finding people to help. Fond memories arise of going to my aunt's house next door assisting her with chores or cleaning my cousin's bedroom for one cent. It wasn't the most profitable business venture, but my time was not about the money. For me, it was *always* about relationships and searching to belong.

My aunt would play music and do "the bump" with me. Now I am super aging myself, but "the bump" was where you would stand side-by-side and bump your hips together with the music. Being a bit shorter than my aunt I would have to jump as I bumped—an entertaining picture I am sure—but the relational aspect of this engagement together was life altering for me.

My cousin, who I just mentioned, would take the time to teach me a song on the piano or drive me in his car as he was practicing for his road test. I remember not being able to see over the front dash of that blue Dodge Dart and loved it when he did 360s over and over. This older cousin would stop his world to spend small amounts of time with his little cousin. These memories were special. They were life altering and gave my out-of-balance world small moments of meaning, worth, and value.

I felt loved.

I needed more.

God wanted more for me and from me.

This sophomore chapel service required much introspection and self-reflection to ascertain what was happening to me. Why did these questions drive me to tears? I knew God was "in my heart." Jesus loved me, and the Holy Spirit's presence lived with me still, so what was going on? I was a decently successful "good girl." My life was full of rules-to-follow and I diligently worked hard at being compliant.

The funny thing is my focus was normally on being good. My rule breaking was often the result of either ignorance or exhaustion. It is difficult to follow so many rules. Sometimes it felt like the rules had rules. If I did cross the line, it was not very far and certainly not for very long. The internal guilt alone I experienced from crossing the line was unbearable. I remember one trip to downtown Boston I watched a pair of jugglers throwing items to each other and observed how they kept everything in the air. It was astonishing the number of different things they could juggle without dropping. The pressure to be good was comparable to a professional juggler and I felt like I was the opposite of these professionals. The number of rules to follow and the inability to successfully juggle them all, left me feeling like a continual failure.

By tenth grade I had a tremendous amount of Bible knowledge from church and private school, but I was not successfully juggling the rules and keeping all these expectations in the air. It seemed the more rules thrown at me, the more I felt I was a failure, which added to my already low self-esteem. At this point in my life, my identity was primarily wrapped up in being a daughter, granddaughter, and sibling and my purpose was to be obedient—which psychologically and emotionally deemed me a regular failure.

I was juggling what everyone else thought was right (people-pleaser, remember?). What I needed was to engage in what the Bible referred to as "right living."

RIGHT LIVING

Reading to understand the first chapter of the book of Romans would have helped at this young age. I understood that I had a personal purpose and calling for my life—to be obedient. Romans chapter one tells me that I am called an apostle and I was chosen to tell Christ Jesus's story. I did not realize at that age I was experiencing two conflicting disconnects. The first disconnect was between the Bible's instruction to me and what many of my Christian elders were telling me my actions should be (usually in the form of a command). The second disconnect was finding a gap between the actions or behaviors of those same Christian elders who were working to advise and correct what was wrong in my life versus the Bible's instructions for right living.

What I did know at this age was that I needed to improve my actions and pursue the biblical idea of "right living." So, I continued my journey, determined to better strive to seek and understand God's calling for my life while juggling the instructions of others (my elders) around me. My intentions and heart were pure, along with the knowledge that God makes people right with himself through faith.[1] What I was not understanding in this phase of life was that I was made right with God by following *his* standards, not other people's belief or opinion of what God's standards were. I needed to find my own faith. Even though I grew up in an environment where following the rules was priority number one, I continued to learn and strive toward "right living."

I wanted to strive.

I knew God's promises and did not stop believing. I wanted to grow stronger in my faith and sought a life that was actively living right with God.[2] Tears flowed at my sophomore chapel service because I knew my current life was not in sync with God's expectations of me, and my actions needed adjustments. God got my attention, and I became more serious about desiring to please God.

The fifth chapter of the book of Romans teaches that the result of living right with God is inner peace, happiness, joy in spite of trouble, hope, and love. I needed more of this in my life. I wanted a deeper relationship with God. I was searching for intimacy. I still needed to belong. Knowing that God was with me, this next chapter of my life was the beginning of a new understanding that salvation was just a starting point —my old self needed to step aside. At the age of five, I asked Jesus into my heart, and at this age of sixteen, I rededicated my life, aiming to honor God with my words, attitudes, and actions. I no longer wanted sin to control my thoughts but wanted to obey God and live a life that was pleasing to him—engaging my "new self." The old things should pass away and I was to become a new creation.[3] I was someone beautiful that God adored.

Striving to find balance, it was still difficult to decipher what others said pleased God and what God stated pleased him, but I continued moving forward. I was growing. I knew I was not alone—God was with me, and he loved me. I also realized that knowing about God was not enough. God wanted more from me. God wanted relationship. My bearings were set and off I went into life again—until college.

Chapter Two
CONTINUING CONCERNS

Have you ever wondered why you do the things you do not want to do and seem to fail to do the things that you want?[1]

This is how I felt in this stage of my life. I mentioned at the end of the last chapter that life went on "until college," so your mind may have speculated about all the bad behaviors and naughtiness that must have ensued. Come on, a girl who grew up sheltered on "a compound" with limited secular social experiences—there is much trouble to get into without adult supervision, right? Nope! I continued to be that "good girl". Thankfully, my tenth-grade chapel experience added the drive to please God with my life.

Attending a Christian college, I was excited to have a larger social setting and a wider pool to find new friendships, relationships, and connection opportunities. Did that happen? Nope! Most of the students around me were interested in drinking, bad habits, and/or sexual relationships that I did not dare engage in because I did not want to displease God. I found myself alone again. So, I changed colleges—one of the best choices in my life—and finished my undergrad in Palm Beach, Florida.

Yes—sand, sunshine, and warmth! My grades soared upward, my attitude improved, and my desire for self-care increased. I joined my older sister at this institution. She was interested in spiritual living, and my life began finding a better balance.

I was thankful to God for so many great things he was doing in my life. So why was it that in the last semester of my senior year the flow of tears started again and my emotional world came crashing down? I thought I was happy, striving to honor God, pleasing my elders, helping those around me, and verbally asking God to use my life. God was using me in miraculous situations. So why was I having trouble continuing forward? Why the breakdown and tears?

The first reason for this breakdown was my heart's desire to follow the path that God wanted for me. I was seeking my identity, purpose, and worth; I knew God wanted to use me, but I was still discovering what that looked like. I knew God had a bigger, special purpose for my life. I was seeking God's desire. Memorizing scripture through the years, Proverbs 3:5-6 was a description of where my journey was in this moment of time. "Trust in the Lord with all your heart; do not depend on your own understanding. Seek his will in all you do, and he will show you which path to take." For years I trusted in the Lord, tried to depend on him and seek him, but I was not inspired to do it with *all* my heart. I was not sure what "all my heart" really meant at this age of twenty-two, but I was desperately seeking and asking God to use me. Years of seeking and trying to find the path that God wanted for me, I was learning that the answers for me were found in scripture. Proverbs 3:5-6 told me to seek and trust in the Lord and verse seven commanded me to fear the Lord and turn from all evil actions.

Fear was an attribute that I was familiar with.

As a child, I feared disobeying my father. One example of fear and direct obedience was when I first received my driver's license. My father instilled a distinct fear of getting a ticket for speeding. The serious conversation my father and I had when I first began to drive was that if I got pulled over and got a speeding ticket, he would take my driver's license away. Now me being an independent, out-of-the-nest social spirit, one of the last things I wanted to do was lose my freedom and ticket to civilization. So, whenever I was tempted to make an unwise choice behind the wheel of a car, I did not. My fear of the discipline of my earthly father outweighed the desire to make a poor driving choice.

Cruise control was my friend. In fact, if one of my cars did not come with cruise control, I had it installed, along with a sunroof. The sunroof was another requirement for me needing to allow the sunshine into my life whenever possible.

The fear of getting a speeding ticket is still with me today. I remember getting pulled over when early married and subconsciously afraid that my father was going to punish me by taking away my license. I was often punished as a child for failing to juggle all the rules, and the fear of disappointing was and is deeply instilled in me. I am thankful for this. Yes, the fear ethic may have been a bit on the excessive side at times, but the result was constructive. I'm a woman who did not become sexually active, afraid she would be the one getting pregnant before marriage. I stayed out of many troubles that a lot of my peers did not. Unfortunately, the "good girl" mantra and the continual drive for spiritual growth resulted in social segregation, and a lack of connectedness with others. Another downside is the excessiveness of fear spilled out into other areas of my life. Fear became a part of my identity. I was afraid of people not liking me, of being misunderstood, and cared too much what people thought about me which led to unhealthy levels of low self-esteem.

I was unaware I was spending so much energy being afraid of so many things. It wasn't until adulthood that I learned fear can be healthy when focused in the right direction. Fear was familiar and I was ignorant of its dysfunction in my life. I was realizing these fears that had become part of my identity were greater than my fear of God. I embraced the loving God, merciful God, caring and forgiving God, but I didn't have a healthy fear of God. I was reading scripture for myself and was realizing I was choosing which portions I wanted to embrace and pay attention. Obeying God was still not my first priority.

Failure to fear God results in a disconnect between belief, attitude, and actions. Many of my elders used to say, "Do as I say, not as I do." They modeled for me a self-directed faith—being obedient to God in a way that works for me. Self-directed faith picks and chooses what instructions from God's word to listen to and apply to life. Here is an example. My mother drove my sisters and myself to piano lessons every week. I didn't mind playing piano if I could play the songs that interested me. The basics: scales, runs, and chords were not fun to play. So, my practice time was spent rushing through the basics with the least amount of effort or focus so I could get to playing the songs I enjoyed.

My focus during my piano-lessons years was about what I wanted to get out of it rather than what I wanted to invest. I went through all the motions my piano teacher instructed, but my results were not evident of someone taking ten plus years of piano lessons. This personally-driven intentional attitude is like self-directed faith and it spilled into other areas of my life. In college, if there were classes I enjoyed, I got good grades, but if I did not find the class interesting or if the material was too difficult, I put in less effort with the hope of simply passing. I applied myself enough to appear "obedient," but the result often fell short of all I could have been.

Unfortunately, I also took this approach with God and reading his word. I focused on what I enjoyed in scripture and spent the least amount of effort engaging in the parts that were more difficult or uninteresting. I love music, so most of my spiritual interaction was spent listening to music and worshipping God through song. I told myself I was obedient to all scripture and believed my intentions were pure, but when I self-assessed, I questioned why I was still seeking answers and falling short of all I knew God said I could be.

Why did I still wrestle within?

Why did I allow others to take priority over what God wants for me?

I had no expectation of perfection, but I should have been more mature. I needed to place greater value in my relationship with God, and less on the fear of disappointing others. With over ten years of scripture, teaching, and biblical theology under my belt, I should have better mastered the spiritual basics. My relationship with God is like any other relationship, I must put in if I expect to get back. I realized that I wanted more out of the relationship than I was investing.

I was seeking God's desire for my heart and wanted to follow the path that *God* wanted for me. As a college graduating senior, I needed to seek and trust God with *all* my heart. I also needed to value God's view of me over others' opinions. I was learning that God's opinion is what truly matters—*my* identity, purpose, and worth are defined by God.

The second reason for this senior year breakdown was my internal health. I shared earlier that I had buried mental, sexual, and emotional abuse deep inside—with most of the memories blocked from my psyche. I thought at the time, that burying memories was the only way to persevere, keep a happy spirit, be an encouragement to others, and have positive memories. However, God wanted to use me for his good, and he also wanted to heal me for my good. God needed to help me work through and dispose of many brutal incidents, so the things done to me would no longer inhabit me, burden me, or define me. By facing and releasing my past, God began rebuilding me from the inside out, restoring me into the person he created me to be.

I attended many outside church services in sunny Palm Beach that senior year at a venue called "Chapel by the Lake." God's word began activating deep inside me. At this serene spot, God began calling me to live with him 100 percent and began healing my insides. Proverbs 4:20–27 describes this new journey God was taking me on. God wanted my *whole* self. God wanted me to trust him with my *whole* heart and lean on his understanding, not mine. God wanted me to have health for my *whole* body—my mind, my soul,[2] my relationships. God was calling me closer to him and my response was to regularly go to this beautiful Chapel-by-the-Lake setting with its bright sunshine and peaceful blue water and allow myself to cry, wail, and heave the painful past from my insides out.

This painful, confusing, time was when I realized on a deeper level that I was not alone, but God was with me, cared for me, loved me, and desired me. These days and hours were spent bonding with God at this beautiful, safe place. I found that with God, I belonged. God did not only want to live in my heart, as my young theology heard, he wanted to be part of my whole self, my life, and that is exactly where I wanted him to be—needed him to be. I didn't want this to be a one-time event in my life. I wanted this closer relationship with God to continue.

The words shared in Proverbs chapter 4 were key to finding health for the whole self. Solomon, the writer of the book of Proverbs shared that I was to pay attention, listen closely, and not forget God's words.

I needed to *let* God work in and through me.

Solomon explained that only some will understand that these words from God are the key to controlling our thoughts, mouths, focus, and actions to continue strong. I was on a new path to find what God wanted for me, and for my life. I needed to listen closely. I needed to pay attention. I needed to not forget. I needed to hold on. I wanted to keep God's commands. God's words are key to life for those who find them, and I wanted to be one of those people scripture talked about who experience a "full life." At this stage, I did not know what a "full life" was like, but I knew that I wanted it. The result of this Chapel-by-the-Lake experience was a feeling of being free. I was no longer heavy, confused, or searching for meaning in life. I was comforted, cared for, and thankful for a calmness and peace that trumped all I could have ever imagined. I wanted to linger in this experience, but knew life was going to move on.

Knowing graduation was around the corner followed by heading home to Syracuse, New York, it was imperative that God needed to help me face my past to persevere in the present. Fears from my past needed to take a back seat. My young theology was transforming, and God was beginning a new work in me.[3] The old was becoming new. What I gained from my formative years was awareness of who I was obeying. God needed to be my first priority. I knew God had a bigger purpose for my life, and I was discovering that purpose.

My energy at this point couldn't be wasted on asking myself "could I continue," because I wanted to continue. I needed to continue. I had belief but knew this belief needed to be activated in a new way. God intended the best for me and knew my journey forward would not be easy.

Listening to God through scripture was the next step for me. Better listening to God was key to activating my life so that I could do what God was calling me to do.

God helped me continue.

Next thing I knew, I was caught smack dab in the middle of midlife.

SECTION 2

Active Belief

ACTIVE BELIEF

Midlife is an interesting time.

At the age of thirty-seven, my gal doctor announced to me that I was in post menopause (meno).

Seriously?

Desperately praying for God to provide me with a baby since I was twenty-four, I was immediately thrown into deep distress. All I knew about post meno was that I was not able to have children—no chance for pregnancy. For many women not having babies might be a relief, but for me, walking out of the doctor's office that day, I was numb and in shock after hearing what seemed like the worst thing that could be spoken into my life. My goals in life—most people don't know this—were to sing and have babies. Many, many babies would be a plus. There was and still is an urging inside of me to be a part of the miraculous experience of a life growing within me.

Hearing the finality of this news put me immediately on a quest for answers, and the professionals didn't have any. The only information given was my low estrogen level, missing menstrual cycle, and the words "post menopause." What did that mean? My menstrual cycle ended when my first stepson moved in permanently, and I explained to the doctor that I believed my body was just responding to stress—they disagreed. Their diagnosis later did not make sense in my early forties, when I began experiencing, what I now know were perimeno symptoms—extreme vaginal dryness, irritability, and weight gain. Ugh— I experienced a slow and steady increase in weight around my stomach area. The "midlife middle" could not be stopped no matter what effort was put in with diet and exercise.

Unfortunately, a decade ago, there was not much information available on the midlife woman, which is one reason why I am a midlife expert today. I don't want to get ahead of myself, so let's hang here for another minute. The news that my ovaries had died, and my body was no longer able to carry a baby, put my world into a tailspin. Now, I was thankful for my stepsons, *but* I always believed that birthing children was one of the key purposes for my life.

Now what?

My response to this midlife crisis was to focus on taking care of everyone around me. Knowing God was with me, had an unrevealed purpose for my life, and wanted the best for me, I tried to continue forward and be thankful for the things I had. During the next eight years we had the blessing of all three stepsons living with us permanently. My boys were dealing with brokenness, so I focused on patiently loving them—no matter the cost. My husband, with a much-needed career change, began a full-time academic path, so it was up to me to financially provide for the family. This began my adventure in the insurance industry. I received an opportunity that promised to "take my soul" working six to seven days a week, and I accomplished what I set out to do—financially provide for my family by unfortunately working eighty plus hours a week. I was successful, won awards, and quickly achieved a high six-figure income.

But all this came at a cost.

The cost was my health and wellbeing.

My stress increased along with my meno cortisol levels, and my body got so heavy that my arches fell. I was having difficulty just walking to the mailbox. I became what I refer to as a "cart-leaner." I was unable to walk around the grocery store without having a shopping cart to lean on.

Physically, I was incapacitated. At forty-five years old, I was obese with exceptional dietary habits. My food intake was healthy whole foods and did not include snacking, sugars, or caffeine. My favorite liquid was water, I was constantly active with plenty of movement, and my spiritual life was commendable. Unfortunately, the stress from my job was extreme due to financial responsibilities along with having few hours left after the work week to spend quality time with anyone, so I was left feeling alone, unappreciated, unworthy, and entangled with no escape. This feeling of entrapment left me living minute-by-minute, asking God to help me get through my day.

My life was out of my control.

I felt empty, alone, and wanted to better balance my life.

Lower levels of estrogen came with, what I refer to as "clearer thinking." I knew at this point in my life that I *needed* to take care of myself. Unfortunately, taking care of me felt like selfishness, which made this life change difficult. I knew God was with me—he demonstrated his presence daily. Still, I was at a place in my life where I began to cry again. Heaving, bawling, deep tears from within. These tears flowed in my car before walking into my workplace and then again when I arrived home late in the evening before I walked into the house. I felt trapped and there did not seem to be any escape. There had to be more to life. More to what God purposed for me. I knew I was missing something and desperately needed to find it.

My response and only hope was God. I decided to dive even deeper into reading the Bible and asking, pleading with God to reveal himself to me, to save me, to come to my rescue with my obese body, low self-esteem, and broken confidence. God met me where I was. I took another step forward trusting God with my life and continued to ask for minute-by-minute guidance.

God continued to show up in miraculous ways.

I met a coach to help me lose weight until I could safely exercise, was offered employment working weekdays nine to five, and received a calling from God to work with women while attending a Beth Moore simulcast (Beth Moore is an inspiring women's leader and teacher.) I purchased a Bible study from Beth

Moore, *Jesus, 90 Days with the One and Only,* and my life began to turn a corner. I listened to God's calling and started a small women's Bible study at my house, began leading a women's ministry at church, and over the next ninety days my belief in God flourished. I began to call God my "main man." *God was all that was important.* I turned our spare bedroom into a Bible study room and placed pictures of my wedding day on the wall in front of my comfy brown, reclining chair. I began praying for my marriage. I married an amazing man, but years of struggle drew us apart, so I began trusting God to handle my spouse, me, and our relationship.

Who better to lean on and fix what had become broken?

I began praying for my stepsons and asking God to help me feel important in their lives. I kept praying for myself. The years of "stuffing" had become emotional "scar tissue" that made it hard for me to receive love and be empathetic to others. I continued praying for the call God had placed on my life to encourage women.

My belief in God was primarily based on what my "young theology" taught me about God, but my current study was challenging me that my belief was inactive. *Inactive* means "unused, inoperative, dormant, or unworking."[1] There was a disconnect. While reading John chapter 14, God began stirring within me recognition that my belief lacked movement. God was calling me to have what I refer to as an "active belief." What do I mean by "*active* belief?" The word *active* means "alive, effective, operating, and functioning."[2] So, simply put, my belief needed to be alive, effective, operating, and functioning. I was re-awakened to what Jesus *did* at the cross and began to living a changed life because of Christ, becoming more like Christ, and living better for Christ. This could only be done with the Holy Spirit's guidance.

Chapter Three
RE-AWAKENING

Have you experienced any of the midlife changes yet?

Have you heard the nightmare stories and stigmas?

This uncelebrated chapter in our lives, midlife meno, is a change in women with very little understanding. This important transition from young adult life to older adulthood that generally spans a third of woman's years inspired me to return to get a master's and better educate myself at the age of forty-eight. It was only three years later that the first Midlife Mutiny Workshop was birthed to help share more information with women about this natural transition.

Through this event, the women united and together turned stigmas into esteem. For many, it was an awakening. I was able to inspire and help women see that midlife is a new steppingstone, an opportunity to begin again, and not a road to the end.

This event was inspiring to me too. With my children grown and an empty nest, I had the opportunity to stop and assess myself, my relationships, and my use of time.

Midlife is a new steppingstone, a beginning point, and a chance of opportunity!

So, what prompted this self-assessment?

My last couple decades had been consumed with taking care of everyone around me, except me. I experienced an "ah-ha" moment when my middle son asked me "What do you like or like to do?" My upcoming birthday spurred my son's desire to know me better, but his question stumped me. It had been so many years since I had thought about my desires, dreams, goals, and aspirations. My life was wrapped up in being a mom, wife, daughter, a servant at church, and again taking care of everybody but myself. It had been a long time since I considered what I liked. My response took some deep thought and recollection. I replied, "I love the water, waterskiing, and soccer." His swift response was, "We never do any of those things." He was right. It was clear that I needed to resuscitate my dreams.

Who had I become?

I was more than a mom, wife, daughter, sister, and I needed to dream again. To imagine myself differently and believe in myself so I could live to my full potential—whatever that meant. God called me to encourage women. I needed to lead by example. To lead women to their full potential, I needed to find mine.

I was on a mission to *determine, discover, dream, decide*, and then *do*. *(One of my coaching concepts.)*

DETERMINE

One midlife advantage I already mentioned is that with lowering estrogen comes what I refer to as "clearer thinking" and a refreshing new perspective. Yes, maybe I find myself a bit more aggressive or blunt at times, but enough energy has been wasted and it is a new season to become, to be, and to move forward.

> ***Do you have a memory of a time in your life when you drew a line in the sand and said,***
>
> ***"I'm moving forward. I might not know where I am going, but it is not back to where I came from!"***

I set my mindset and continued to dive into God's word to learn and grow. I needed to explore his word with the help of the Holy Spirit. While reading Galatians chapter 3, I was inspired to rely on the Holy Spirit's power to make my life complete. This is something I couldn't do using my own power. My life was very similar to the people from Galatia. They accepted God, received the helper (Holy Spirit), and then tried to complete their salvation by using their *own* power. Scripture's reply was, "How foolish." When we do life in our own strength and we don't engage with the Holy Spirit, the result is never right behavior. It's a holy paradox. I can do the right thing and still be wrong if I'm doing it apart from the Holy Spirit.

I knew I should not move forward alone, but I needed to continue. I could only move forward with supernatural power. With the Holy Spirit's power, I could live by faith and discover who God wanted me to be. I continued to seek God's purpose and calling for my life. It was decided, it was settled, and with the help of the Holy Spirit, nothing was going to stand in my way.

DISCOVER

This mission involved exploration, self-analysis, and introspection, which began by first identifying what type of person I was and who I wanted to become. I loved helping people, and was a professional people pleaser, but needed to engage in better self-care so that God could effectively use me. I needed to be healthier to fulfill my calling to encourage women. I needed to engage in better self-care so that I could encourage women to do the same.

My exploration later revealed to me that I needed to be a "Titus 2 woman." I needed to have an older woman mindset, a more mature mindset. I needed to control my tongue, live in moderation, be spirit controlled, live with integrity, and find like-minded ladies with whom to pursue life. I needed to surround myself with people who were trying to live right, have faith, love, peace, and trust in the Lord with pure hearts.

While reading the fourteenth and fifteenth chapters of the book of Matthew, I learned that Jesus was exposed to many needy people. In this story, one of Jesus's friends had died and Jesus needed to go to a quiet place to be alone—Jesus demonstrated self-care. On his way to the mountain to pray, Jesus encountered a group of people who needed him, so he stopped and was attentive to their needs, but later that day continued to the mountain top to spend alone time with God, again demonstrating self-care. It was inspiring to see how Jesus balanced self-care with others' care. I began to spend quiet time with God, reading and praying at the mountain top, while asking for help with the never-ending heartaches and difficult times that continued to come my way.

My young theology was now a base theology, a foundation on which to build. God had my attention. My young theology taught me that Jesus was coming back some day to take me to heaven, but Jesus was not just in my physical heart. Diving into the Greek offered the expanded understanding that the word "heart" meant Jesus was living in my whole self, until he comes again. I needed to have an active belief, truly believing Jesus was the way, truth, and life and resting in his promises.[1] I was discovering that when I gave God more control over my "whole-self," difficult experiences would still ensue, but I would not be disappointed. I would experience joy, peace, and success in life regardless of the circumstances.

I had my same base theology but was experiencing different results.

I was figuring out what God wanted me to do with every minute of every day. My activated belief inspired action, and this earthly dynamic duo (the Holy Spirit and me) began allowing God to do his work in and through me. The quality of my care was increased when empowered by the Holy Spirit.

I was finding where I fit into God's plan.

I was discovering my identity and purpose in God.

I was confident, trusting God to counter my fears and self-doubt.[2]

I was ready to ask myself:

Am I doing what I want for God?

Am I doing what I've done my entire young adulthood?

or

Am I living as God wants me to live?

Put simply, is my life actually pleasing to God?

God tells us what he wants from us. Right living means allowing the Holy Spirit to empower our obedience to his direction. I realized this in an issue of daily discovery

Am I doing what God requires of me today or am I doing what I want to do *for* God? Maybe this example will clarify what I'm trying to say here.

Have you ever had someone offer you a gesture or do something kind for you, but it was nothing you prefered? Maybe they gave you a gift that was "not your style" or preference?

I had a girlfriend who would give me beautiful country-style gifts because she *loves* the country flair. I am not drawn to country style décor, so her heartwarming gifts left me in a predicament. My initial reaction opening the gift was thankfulness, followed by slight anxiety wondering what I should do with it. She is sweet to think of me and offer me a gift, but I don't want to display it in my house. To be honest I don't want it at all.

My emotions were mixed because she bought me a gift without me in mind.

For years, I would display or use these gifts from people who either didn't know me or didn't care about my preference. They were nice people who would do nice things for me for their own benefit. This is what the Israelites did to God in Micah chapter 6. God loved and cherished these Israelites, but they did their own thing. They worshiped God the way *they* wanted to. These Israelites were doing good things, but not doing what God asked, not doing what pleased God. They weren't doing with *God* in mind.

The attitudes of the Israelites provoked deeper self-discovery and posed some additional life questions:

Was I offering my life to God in a way that was pleasing to him?

Did my behaviors demonstrate that I knew God?

I began seeking to know God deeper. It was only after I set my determination and began accepting that God personally knew me, had me in mind, and wanted the best for me, that I was able to start dreaming again.

DREAM

As a coach, I am sadly amazed by the expression on a woman's face after asking her about her desires, dreams, and goals. Very often I get a blank stare. Many women have not taken the opportunity to discover themselves and are busy being who everyone has demanded them to be. Through the years, dreams tend to get lost or left on the wayside.

Why is it that getting caught up in the hustle and bustle of life can cause us to lose our aspirations, our goals, or our dreams?

What have you always wanted to do, to be?

Regardless of where you are today, it is time to begin dreaming or continue dreaming about the opportunities you have in life. This world needs you! Unless you step into your purposes in this life, those around you are missing out.

Ephesians 2:10 teaches that God made me who I am, in his image and for his purposes. This passage reminded me that Christ died so I could live my life to its fullest. I was designed with God's purpose, and I should continue forward in that purpose. Why wouldn't I want a full life? Again, I had to pause and ask myself, am I doing that for which I am purposed?

As I shared earlier, I aspired to be a mom and singer. Always an active lady, I loved athletics, helping people, and social settings. My aging body pushed aside my dream to carry a baby within and the thrill of slalom waterskiing should be a memory to be cherished, but the singing, helping others, and creating safe encouraging social spaces for midlife women is still to be experienced and something to which I aspire. I was daring to dream.

I was drawn to the word "aspire" when creating a workshop a few years back.

Aspire *means* to *"dream, crave, pursue, strive, and yearn for something."*[3]

Yes, some things will never come to fruition, but there is so much opportunity, and there is much to get done. I was and still am a woman in midlife with so much ahead of her. So much potential. So much to do. So many women to impact. Women to equip, empower, and encourage.

While reading 1 Peter, I was energized and began dreaming. This passage stated there was a call and command for my life. I needed to commence, move forward, and get going. The call was to holy living. God wanted my whole self—mind, body, and spirit to be blameless.[4] The command was to love God and others. I was to show respect to all people.[5] Once I determined and discovered, I was to begin. I was to strengthen myself with God's way of thinking so I could live on earth doing what *God* wants.[6] I needed to think clearly and control myself so that I could pray more effectively. If words came out of my mouth, they should be words from God. If I was to serve others, I was to serve with God's strength without complaining so that God could be praised in all that I did. The most important instruction was to love others deeply.

More than anything, my dreams were turning into a drive to make a change, to do something different. I decided, I needed to keep learning, growing, and moving forward.

DECIDE

Have you ever set your mind to something, and it doesn't happen? Like: I want to lose weight, help a friend, eat healthier, or exercise? We are all on our own journey, but we all live in this busy, messy world that can keep us from our true desires, dreams, and destinies. Dealing with the midlife middle, continual financial responsibilities, typical aging body challenges, and the world's drama caused enough stress in life that I found that even though I determined, discovered, and began to dream, something more had to happen for me to experience the success that I was hoping for, longing for, and desperately needed. I decided to move into the person that I was created to be.

Earlier I mentioned being in my mid-forties and struggling with weight gain while engaging in healthy eating and regular movement. My weight had gotten to almost 300 pounds and for three years I decided that enough was enough. I adjusted my diet to eating only organic, cut out any processed foods, no snacking, very little sugar, no late-night eating, zero caffeine, and always drinking lots of water. At this point in my life, I decided to get my body healthier and to a safer weight. I was determined, but without the help of a coach I was not able to help myself. I had mastered helping others, but not helping *me*. Helping *me* felt selfish. A coach helped me focus within so I could transform my without. My thoughts needed to change. I didn't feel worthy of anything, or anyone. I'm not sure how I got to this place of unworthiness. Yes, there were years of sibling banter stating that I was "ugly," "stupid," "adopted," and I'm sure more stored negative memories, but why did these things stay with me and change the core of who I was? Hiring a health coach was pivotal with my journey because I had decided where my life was going, and it was different this time. I had allies.

This time I tried to have different behavior than God's people of Israel. After Moses led God's people out of captivity, the people would trust God, then get distracted from God and begin complaining and practicing bad behavior. God would answer and provide, and soon they were distracted again, and these behaviors went round and round. As I have shared, my life was like that. I accepted God at age five, then went on with life. I re-dedicated my life at age sixteen, and then life continued on auto-pilot. God got ahold of me my senior year in college, then I found myself in my mid-forties obese, overworked, burned out from helping others, dealing with meno, and looking ahead at my life wondering if I was going to be wheelchair bound moving forward.

Limiting distractions, I was learning to listen to God and trying to obey what *he* was saying to me. Something new God was teaching me was that I needed to love myself. Using a coach to help me physically, I realized that my mental and emotional self also needed assistance. I lost seventy pounds in a short period of time and was able to safely exercise. I decided to move forward with a coach's help, and I was successful. Together we set my determination, we discovered "why" I wanted to lose the weight, dreamed about how life would feel once I lost the weight, decided to begin, and then we did—together. This "together" teamwork inspired me.

Like God's people of Israel, I had successes in my life. God provided. But before I knew it, life felt like it was spiraling out of control in one of the areas (mind, body, spirit.) I had decided to have different behavior, but balancing these three areas was difficult. Reading the book of Isaiah, I began to understand what God said his people did that displeased him and what he required of them. The prophet Isaiah relayed that God was telling his people that yes, they were worshipping God with their mouths and honoring him with their lips, but their hearts were far away from him. They were basing their worship on human rules. These people were making their own plans with their lives, not asking God for help, and making decisions without the help of the Holy Spirit or asking God first. These people were bringing God sacrifices and offerings, and praying to him while going through what I refer to as "spiritual motions." God's reply was, "Who asked you to do all this running about?" God said they were not loyal to him, did not know him, did not understand him, and he called them worthless. They were worthless because they were refusing to obey what God's specific instructions were. They were busy doing *for* God and not doing *with* God. God wanted them to listen and obey his specific commands. God wanted them to pay attention to *him* and not be so busy with their daily lives.

Reading the book of Isaiah grabbed my attention. Spending decades involved in Christian ministry and striving to honor God with my life, I now needed to test my faith, my life, and my intentions.

How much "running about" had I been doing?

How much of my service to God would he consider worthless?

Was I living *for* God or was I living with the help of the Holy Spirit to bring honor and glory to God?

My first reaction to these deep questions was to justify my behaviors. With a busy life and time being a rare commodity, would God really think my service to him was worthless activity? This pushed against what society teaches us about our time, effort and self-importance. Can you imagine me coaching a working professional trying to balance work, job, family, relationships, and self-care, stating that her expended energy was worthless? Now I'm not negating that we can feel worthless, but communicating these words would most likely mean that l wouldn't have that client for very long. God had my attention again.

It took some introspection for this new concept of worthiness to sink in to me. I've shared my journey to feel worthy and the desire to live a beneficial, fruitful, important, meaningful, productive, significant, worthwhile, and helpful life.

I did not want God to call me worthless.

So, I decided to listen and hear what God was communicating.

If God was sharing what *he* wanted, why not listen? Why would I waste my energy and time doing something different? Listening to what God wanted me specifically to do sounded like a shortcut to get that which I was searching for. God was re-awakening me.

Deciding to make a life change or experience altered results generally involves making different choices with mindfulness. I needed to assess my options.

When coaching professional women, or even mothers with demanding roles and responsibilities, it is important to assess their choices, behaviors, habits, and the usage of their time. What we usually discover together is that we spend a lot of time "running about," spinning in circles, or caught on autopilot and need to brainstorm time-efficient solutions to get the desired results. That might include making different choices or engaging in different behaviors—especially right behaviors.

Isaiah states that the path of life is level for those who are right with God. The Lord makes life smooth for people who are right with him, so they will complete the things that *God wants* them to do.[7] God wants us to listen and obey because he wants to help take care of us. Isaiah shares that God helps people who trust in him, who enjoy doing good, and who remember how *God* wants them to live.[8] God also wants to receive the glory. *(This pushes against the belief that God helps those who help themselves.)* When we engage in right living, anyone who sees us will know we are people that the Lord has blessed, and our lives will bring God glory.[9]

My journey led me to re-discover my destiny and continue striving to seek God's will for my life. I decided I was moving forward to my destination and needed to do that with intentionality. My life of intention needed to move forward with the help of the Holy Spirt, every day.

Chapter Four
INTENTIONALITY

An accurate display of the word "intention" is not authentically modeled by the world around us. Our society has mastered the "gift of good intentions."

What do I mean by this?

Have you ever had someone say, "I was going to get you this for your birthday" or "I was going to call you to go out last weekend" or "I wanted to ___, but ___ *(you add in the excuse/reason)*." They might even show up late to help with a project after all the work is completed saying, "I was going to help!" Our culture has deemed that verbalizing something you want or planned to do is the same action as doing it. It's not!

This is what I refer to as a *gift of good intentions*. "I would have" is not the same as I *did*.

Isaiah, Jeremiah, Micah, and Joel all include the message that God is not very happy with the *gift of good intentions*. To combat the problem of *good intentions,* God asks his people to listen to his instruction, obey his commands, and return to him with their *whole* heart (mind, body, spirit). God is glorified when we imitate him day after day in and through our lives. God desires intentionality that results in action.

The word intention means "act or determine mentally some action or result.
Intentionality is a purpose or action
that effects one's action or conduct."[1]

I set my intention to use the help of a coach and took part in a program to safely lose weight so I could re-engage in movement and continue to get the weight off my body. I listened, trusted, and moved forward day-by-day, step-by-step. My intention was not just a desire, but had action and began to move me from point A toward point B.

Intention spurs action.

We are all on our own individual journeys. I knew God had a specific purpose for my life. He also has a purpose for yours. Even though our journeys are unique, we have connecting points. I was learning that if I live a life pleasing to God, the way God intends me to live, my life can be an inspiration to yours in the same manner that your life can be an inspiration to mine.

I have had many situational friendships through the years. These are people who have come into my life for specific reasons to help walk with me. They are still friends today, but we don't actively engage in day-to-day living. I am very thankful for their friendships and their presence when I needed them the most. When I had to move from my 3,000 plus square foot house to a 400 square foot apartment, God sent me a gal who showed up, helped me with an overwhelming household sale, and then disappeared back to her own life. I believe she was sent from God, because she appeared when I didn't know how I was going to persevere, and she was the perfect personality and person I needed for that situation. God gave me a sweet flight attendant co-worker who showed up in my life and assisted me during circumstances when I needed her the most. She lives across the country now, but God placed her in my life on many occasions to be a specific blessing for specific situations. These are examples of just two ladies who have been inspirational to my walk, my journey. I bet you have a few too!

So, getting back to our topic, how did God want me to be intentional with my life?

Micah chapter 6 shares that God tells us what is good and what he desires from us. God wants us to be righteous, merciful, kind, humble, and obedient. What I learned from this chapter was that I needed to be more than just kind to others, I needed to *love* being kind to them.

Micah chapter 6 left me again asking myself:

Do I treat others fairly?

Do I love who is easy to love, or all people?

How would God reply to my answers?

Am I bringing sacrifices, being thankful, serving God but not listening to him or paying attention to what he is saying to me like his Israelite people mentioned earlier?

The goal of my self-discovery was to assess if my relationship with God was being implemented with good intentions and a good heart, but not what God was asking me to do, be, or become.

Earlier I mentioned people doing kind gestures for me with a personal focus—doing things for me without me in mind. Often in life, I have had situations where someone would buy me lunch or make me food that I did not eat or should not eat. I have a memory in my early adulthood of working with a team to prepare for a children's chorale presentation, having a family member bring me a ham sandwich for lunch, and my girlfriend asking, "Why did she get you ham? You don't even like ham!" I didn't know how to answer that question. It made me ponder the level of relationship I really had.

Reflecting on relationships is important. I have had many relationships with family and friends that would best be described as one-sided. Perhaps *one-sided* is a type of relationship. On many occasions, people have needed me to help them, which is what I lived for. But many these same people are not there for me when I am in need. The one-sided relationship can be damaging. I recall looking back on my life and wondering why people did not want to get to know me? What was wrong with me? Now I ask, why did I assume it was me?

From a young age I had a strong need for attachment and a desire for intimate relationships. I was enlightened while reading *The Search to Belong: Rethinking Inti-*

macy, Community, and Small Groups by Joseph R. Myers who states that very few people have multiple intimate relationships. Myers proposes that most relationships are public and social, and only a few are personal, meaning people who really know you. Myers relational categories explains why it was so difficult for people to be interested in interactive relationship and deep spiritual conversation. Contraposition, while reading the Bible I learned that God desires an intimate relationship with me, a category that Myers states is usually populated by only one or two people. So, I was on a journey to be content with my intimate relationships with God and my spouse. My worth is not based in the number of intimate relationships I form with others.

Shockingly, I realized that the one-sided relationship that frustrated me with others, was the very behavior I was offering to God. God wanted intimacy with me, but I realized that I just wanted to have him near to lean on when life got messy, and I needed his assistance. Micah chapter 6 reminded me again that the Israelites, God's people whom he loved and cherished, did what *they* wanted *for* God. These people felt that by doing good things, keeping from sin, doing good to others, and serving God, God should be pleased with them.

I spent decades offering God a one-sided relationship, where I brought to God what I desired instead of getting to know God and bringing him the things that he would enjoy. I was not *doing* with God in mind. The focus of my intentions began shifting from me to God —a desire to *be* and *do* what he would like. My intention turned to fully seeking God, to find what pleased *him*. When I accepted Christ, my old self was gone, and I became a new creation.[2] By setting my intention with the help of a coach and the Holy Spirit living within me, I started the next phase of my journey— becoming the new, improved person God wanted me to be.

I was seeking God in a new way, exploring who God created me to be.

Pursuing God's specific purposes, I was on a journey with an improved mindset, focus, and intention.

Chapter Five
BECOMING

Have you had a time in your life when you knew that your life was changing for the better?

Maybe you bought your first house and joined the society of homeowners, or you were offered your dream job and could finally get ahead in your finances. The feeling can relate to a dark cloud fleeing from overhead, or even the analogy of watching a sunrise with its bright beautiful oranges and yellows in the morning and knowing that a new day is beginning. This analogy does not particularly mean that the environment changed, or life is now easy, but there is a perspective change. We begin to view ourselves, our lives, in a more positive light because there is something better coming up ahead.

There is a light at the end of the tunnel.
It is a new day.

Do you play cards? My family has always been active card players—they love spending hours playing together. Let me share with you a new perspective I gleaned while playing cards. When I am dealt my initial hand, I have an immediate response to the end result of that particular game. If I'm dealt a wild card or trump cards, I'm excited and anticipating the outcome of that game will be positive. But, if my initial hand does not include any wild cards or trumps, my response is not as up-beat. My confidence in that round of game play is decreased with a lower anticipation of a positive outcome. I still engage in game play, but don't expect to win that game.

My perspective is set when the game begins. My perspective impacts my mood, energy, and sometimes even the outcome both positive and negative.

In life, my perspective (mindset) that I begin each day, each week, or each year with can determine my outcome. My perspective can also determine if I step forward in confidence or not. My point is, given our circumstance in life, the mindset we begin with can determine and affect our success.

> *How we respond to what we are dealt in life*
> *can determine our mindset*
> *and affect the results.*

I was becoming more aware of my mental health and understanding that my thoughts ruled my life.[1] I needed to set my thoughts on things that are good, pleasing, and acceptable. I began understanding that I am still a work-in-progress and that all the ups and downs in life made me who I am. Maybe I am a bit dysfunctional and have more scar tissue than I would like from unfortunate life situations but looking back I know I am who I am today because of my experiences.

I am strong.

I am perseverant.

As Paul wrote in Ephesians four, I was continuing to find my truth in Jesus, leaving my old self behind, being made new in my heart (whole self), and growing into a new person made like God.

While writing this book, I was preparing for a keynote workshop on mental health and the aging mind. I was inspired that even though my gently aging body was producing limitations and my second bout with meno was causing the midlife middle to be stagnant, I needed to shift my focus off these aging limitations and normal life setbacks. With age comes experience, knowledge, understanding, and expertise. With age comes an increase in self-efficacy, which is a person's belief in his or her ability to succeed in a particular situation.[2] With midlife, lower estrogen, and clearer thinking, I needed to focus on the positive. My increase in knowledge, skills, and expertise more than compensate for any aging declines. My increased self-efficacy was re-assuring. I was beginning to see *problems* as challenges to be met, *setbacks* as a reason to double my efforts, and *failure* as a learning experience for the next time.

I was becoming a new, improved version of me.
I was being transformed.

Each day was like watching a beautiful sunrise that filled the dark sky with its radiant beauty. My young theology was maturing, and I was confident that God wanted the best for me. I had determined, discovered, dreamed, and decided that I wanted what God promised for me—and I began to add action. Knowing facilitates doing.

DO

When I became a health coach, we taught "stop-challenge-choose." Before a client decided to eat this or drink that, we advised our clients to stop and ask themselves, "Why do you want to eat 'that?'"

Let's use the example of a cookie. Now I *love* homemade cookies. So, watching my calorie intake and striving to eat food for body fuel, I needed to stop and challenge myself "why" I wanted to eat the cookie. Do I really need the cookie? Is that cookie going to help me further my goal? Then, I would choose whether I eat the cookie or not. My encouragement when coaching clients is that if they choose to eat the cookie, *enjoy it.* Now if my goal is to be a healthier version of myself and put fuel for my body in my mouth, I would need to choose to eat less cookies. Not wanting to weigh 300 pounds again, it is imperative that I stop-challenge-choose anything I desire to put into my mouth, and for me especially, remembering to stop my day and fuel my body. I needed to make good decisions. Physically, my choices needed to move me toward my set goal. Relationally and spiritually, my decisions needed to filter through what God wanted for me and from me.

When reading Jeremiah, I found myself really excited at the advice God shared with his people for making choices. "This is what the Lord said. 'Stand where the roads cross and look. Ask where the old way is and where the good way is and walk on it [the better way.] If you do, you will find rest for yourself.'"[3] This matches up to my coaching philosophy. In all areas of my life, I needed to stop, look both ways, and choose. To choose well, I first need to identify what is the old way and what is the good way, then I can make a good decision. In its application, I see the old way as the things I did in the past that have not led to success.

Choose what is good.

Choose what God says is good and then *go, do,* and *become* with confidence.

Life might not be perfect right now and the timing might not seem exact, but I was learning, and the book of Jeremiah inspired me to be content where God had me. I needed to choose the good way, move forward, and persevere in confidence. This was evolving my *knowing* what I believe into an action step to start *doing* what I believe, allowing others to see God working in and through me. Each step forward, each positive choice between the old way and good way, grows perseverance and is positive forward movement to becoming. My choices dictated my movement either forward or backward. I needed to be careful how I lived my life and choose to use every chance for doing good by listening and obeying.[4] To learn what God wanted me to do, I needed to improve my listening skills.

SECTION 3

Active Listening

ACTIVE LISTENING

If I asked you if you were a good listener, how would you respond?

I have always felt like I am a good listener, but in later years I realized maybe I'm just a safe place or sounding board for people to tell their troubles. Strangers will often tell me about their deepest secrets without me even asking. I shouldn't base my listening skills on the fact that people feel comfortable talking to me. Good listening skills are based on the ability to hear what someone else is saying.

If you asked my mother if I was a good listener, she would most likely explain that of her six children, I was the one who didn't effectively listen. She has often reminisced scenes of wrangling up her kids to run here and there and having to call out my name personally. I needed individual attention and instruction.

In 2015 when I pursued my master's in human services/coaching, I was encouraged to read the book, *Why Don't We Listen Better?* by James C. Petersen. Petersen's book offered me a new perspective on effective listening.

> *"Most people listen, but don't really hear each other"* Petersen shared.
> *"Listening is taking the time to understand each other."*
> This is what Petersen referred to as *"listening deeper."*

His book inspired me to listen differently.

This text encouraged me to *listen to hear, listen to learn,* and *listen to lean* into life to receive results that were greater than I could ever imagine.

I realized I needed to activate my listening skills. As I shared earlier about activating my belief, I needed to heighten my hearing ability. Simply put, I needed to hear in a way that was more alive, effective, operating, and functioning. I needed to listen to people better, and learn to listen to my midlife body. With the lower estrogen streaming through my blood stream and higher levels of cortisol creating havoc, I needed to listen and begin taking better care of myself physically. I needed to keep my stress lower and my cortisol levels regulated. One of the key reasons for my extreme weight gain was not caring for my body. Yes, I ate whole foods, little sugar, no caffeine, no alcohol, and even tried all organic, but what I didn't share was that I repetitively was starving my body. If I wasn't offered a healthy food option, I would not eat. Grabbing a meal at the local gas station was a poor alternative, so lack of eating placed my body in constant starvation mode. So, even the healthy food I finally ate went straight to fat and stored energy.

I even problem solved and began packing meals to go on the road with me. A good plan, right?

Well, combining busy and "me not being a priority," I wouldn't stop to eat the healthy meals I packed for the day. Now I'm not saying that I didn't listen to my body. I did. I knew my body was hungry. I knew I needed to fuel my body with healthy options and understood if I ate processed or fast foods my body would crash or at least not feel very well. Adding midlife challenges to my working environment left my body in a place of toxicity. I was doomed to fail, and my body kept communicating, but I did not choose to stop and listen until my body was in a very desperate state.

Basic mobility became an issue, so I had to stop and listen *differently*. I got to the end of my rope and thought my life had physically ceased. I was incapacitated. I even verbally joked with my husband that I wanted to use the electric wheelchair at the grocery store. It was *too* painful to walk. I realized I needed to listen *differently* to find success in my life and to fully experience the lifestyle I was seeking. I needed to listen to my body and balance hearing what God was speaking to me. I needed to listen *differently*, so I was on a quest to distinguish my listening style.

I continued my journey and began activating my listening skills.

Chapter Six
LISTENING TO HEAR
(Paying attention to understand)

I understood I needed to listen differently to my body and what God was pressing me to do, but I found it hard to focus on myself. I needed to change within. My spiritual health was growing, and I was becoming a better version of my new self in Christ, but I needed to focus on other areas as well. I was striving to develop a better balance, and I was willing to do just about anything to have a better sense of life harmony.

Being desperate, I changed my mental and physical focus to me. For some reason, taking care of myself was perceived as being selfish. Why did I think that self-care was selfish? Where did these ideas come from? Maybe these feelings came from a sense of low self-worth because self-assessment exposed the unworthiness of these basic self-care treatments. I realized I felt guilty spending money on getting my hair cut, buying clothes, and even getting the occasional pedicure. I knew most of my struggle came from my early years of being a people pleaser and obtaining my self-worth from what others thought of me, spoke of me, and how they treated me. Through introspection I discovered I did not like myself. There was still a part of me that was trying to be something else— someone else. But God made me special. Self-care did not have to mean selfish. I wanted to improve.

The battle and struggle began.

It was harder to focus on myself with the unfamiliar moments of silence that emerged. Richard Foster in his book *Celebration of Discipline: The Path to Spiritual Growth* encouraged that silence is not just keeping your mouth shut. Foster stated, "silence always involves the act of listening with God" and being silent makes us feel helpless because we rely on words to manage and control others. Being silent I was able to hear my negative self-talk and obsessive focus on people, the past, and hurts. I was listening to what my psyche was saying to me. I had to listen to realize that I needed to care for me, and that self-care is not wrong in itself.

I remember reading Isaiah chapter 55 when the Holy Spirit distinctively asked me, "Do you have needs?" My internal response was, "Do I ever have needs!" His reply was "Come, listen, listen closely and have a satisfied life. Come if you want to live!" God had my attention. God was urging me to come even closer to listen and hear what he was saying.

Petersen in his listening better book talks about the two different roles and responsibilities of a listener and a talker. The talker's role is to own the problem and explain what most bothers him or her. The listener's role is to be calm enough to hear and not own the problem of the talker. Now, at this point in my walk I was both the listener and the talker. I was talking to myself and trying to listen better to my body. I had begun to own my problems and state what most bothered me. I was better at listening to myself in a calm manner and patiently "cutting myself a break." By beginning to listen to hear better I was helping myself physically, mentally, and socially. Physically I was cutting my body some slack by engaging in loving self-talk. My thoughts began improving and I decided to only surround myself with safe, healthy relationships which dwindled my circle of friends down to an embarrassing few. It was good. It was better. Following a narrow path was taking me to a better place. I was at peace. I was starting to experience internal joy and was thankful.

Growing up, I was taught a Bible story called "The parable of the sower." Reading this parable again as a midlife woman enlightened my aim to listen to hear. Reading this account in three different books: Matthew, Mark, and Luke offered an expanded perspective. Doctor Luke's viewpoint intrigued me because as a doctor he had a shared desire to care for other people's needs.

What is a parable? A *parable* is a "moral story used to teach a principle, truth, or moral lesson."[1] So, this story was about a farmer who decided to go out and scatter seeds. In this narrative, it sounds like this farmer was throwing seed everywhere hoping that they would take root and make plants. As he flung the seeds here and there, some seeds landed on a path, some on rocks, some in thorns and weeds, and others fell on good soil. As expected, the seeds that landed in different areas, had different outcomes. The story continued that the seeds that fell on the path were eaten by birds and the seeds that fell on the rocks had very little soil which caused them to spring up quickly but then get scorched and wither when the sun came up due to lack of rooting. The seed that fell among the thorns and weeds did grow up but got choked out and was not able to yield product. The seed that fell on the good soil grew and produced a crop that multiplied thirty, sixty, and some a hundred times more. Now this parable was used to teach a moral principle. After sharing this story, Jesus stated that people would not listen and learn from it. It was challenged that people will look and look but not learn and will listen and listen and not understand.

I was at a place in my life where I wanted to begin listening to pay attention, hear, and learn. I wanted to listen better. I needed to understand what God was saying to me and asking of me. I wanted to listen and understand with my whole self—mind, body, and spirit—to help with the midlife changes that were challenging me mentally, spiritually, physically, relationally, and socially. Midlife was still a conundrum. As I shared earlier, research and specialists did not offer me information to better understand this phase in life. I personally weathered symptoms of hot flashes, night sweats, vaginal dryness, emotional overwhelm, and weight gain. Why was this happening and what could I do to help myself other than taking medications or hormones? Early meno caught me unaware, and I knew there had to be better communication and non-pharmaceutical strategies. Now back to the parable.

The writer in the book of Isaiah shared that God said, "If they *did* listen and understand, they would come back to me and be forgiven."[2] This parable contained "The secret of the kingdom of God"[3] and I was challenged that "whoever has ears to hear, let them hear."[4]

I wanted to *listen to hear*. I wanted to *listen to learn*. I wanted to *listen to lean in* to what God was saying to me.

So, this story was a parable with a meaning, right? It was a story about a farmer planting seeds freestyle but meant something more than that. Praying to listen to hear so I could begin to listen to learn to understand, I began "chewing on" this passage. I read it over and over.

While reading Doctor Luke's perspective, it was explained that the farmer was God, and the seeds were God's message scattered to people. These people heard God's message and there were different results with this received information.

Wow! I could relate to each of these seedling conditions.

The seed, God's message of salvation, that fell on the road did not even take root because there was no comprehension of acceptance. This is when we hear something and then dispose of it. "Hear" and gone.

There have been numerous times someone tried to give me advice, and depending on the giver I nodded my head, heard what they said, and in-one-ear and out-the-other.

The seed that fell on the rocks was heard and accepted gladly, but when trouble came, it dried up with lack of rooting. This was my spiritual walk many times as a young lady. I would try to honor God and obey, but when life got difficult, I just went back to living how I wanted to live. My life wasn't rooted deep in God. Yes, I knew much about God and the Bible, but those words were not profound in my life and my daily walk. So many times, I heard "the Christian walk is hard," and so many times, I gave in to living an "easier" life. This was living as my old self, not my new self.

The seed that fell on the thorny and weedy soil heard God's message of salvation but allowed circumstances and the environment to choke them out.

Wow. Can you relate to this? The world around us is crazy, unpredictable, and makes it difficult to live the "good way."

The seed that fell on good soil resulted in hearing God's teaching with the heart (mind, body, spirit) and obeying it.

These are different listening styles. All four of these scenarios heard the message. Only one understood, listened to hear with the heart, and obeyed. The others either heard and gave up, heard and allowed others or circumstances to choke them out, or chucked the message all together. I was emboldened to listen to learn and then able to live my life to experience what I was seeking. The condition of my mind, heart, and soul was important if I desired to hear in a way that pleased God. I was excited as I began to listen better so my learning would be enhanced. My hearing was fueling my believing and assisting with my continuing. Learning there were levels of listening, I was inspired to listen better.

My study of Isaiah chapter 55 posed two additional questions beyond "Do you have needs?" These questions were, "Do you want to live?" and "Do you need satisfaction?" Yes, yes, and yes. This passage encourages that we return to God so he will freely forgive us. By returning, we are promised joy, peace, and new growth. Those are three things I very much desired and absolutely needed. I was not only encouraged to return to God, but to come and specifically listen closely to receive blessing, good provision, life, and satisfaction. Who seriously would not want these things? I not only wanted to listen better to hear God, but I also wanted to listen better to learn what I needed to do to obtain these marvelous promises. As I became healthier, I was better able to improve myself and in return help other ladies struggling with life and midlife conditions.

Chapter Seven
LISTENING TO LEARN

I was recently on a trip with some very special ladies. A friend and I took two days off work to drive down and spend some quality time with a sweet lady who tends to work herself to death. The three of us were driving around town bargain shopping, eating local fare, and just enjoying each other's company. We were driving to shop at Ikea—have you been there before? So many bargains and space saving ideas. I was on a quest to buy bath towels, wash cloths, and kitchen towels with built in loops so I could easily hang them to dry. I found some neat, inexpensive gray ones that excited me. It is amazing how simple things can be so temporarily pleasing.

We were driving into the Ikea parking lot when the driver of our car asked if we would like to get dropped off at the front door. I replied "no" and communicated how I valued every minute the three of us had together on this brief thirty-two-hour trip. I was caught me off guard when she pulled up to the front door of the store to drop us off. Perplexed, my mind began to kick into high gear with "if" and "why" questions. *If I communicated I valued every minute together, why would she make a choice that went against that desire? If we value each other, why would she do the opposite of what was expressed? Why even offer a choice if she was going to just do what she wanted anyway?* I was left questioning the level of our relationship over a small situation that occurred driving into a parking lot at an Ikea store. Might sound a bit dramatic, but spending time listening to my body, thoughts, actions, and intentions made me more self-aware and others-aware in day-to-day life interactions.

Being honest, I later had to self-assess how many times I have asked someone for advice and then done the opposite. My husband was certain that when we were first married, I would ask his opinion on something to intentionally do the opposite of his advice. I have caught myself doing this and have needed to self-assess and stop. Subconsciously, something was going on, and it was not healthy behavior if I desired to stay happily married.

Part of being an adult is to make one's own determination. I was learning that I didn't *have* to do what others were telling me to do—I needed to make my own healthy choices. But this arrival to Ikea had me perplexed. I was asked what I preferred, and my special gal friend did the opposite. This felt as simple as asking me if I want vanilla or chocolate ice cream, me answering vanilla, and being handed a chocolate cone. Valuing this friendship, I dared to ask, "Why would you ask and just do the opposite? Why even ask to begin with?" Her response was, "I just thought..." My friend gave an option with no intention of listening or adhering to my response. She had already made up her mind to do it her way but wanted to be nice and offer a choice. Her intention wasn't to cause harm. My friend wanted to be considerate of the two of us ladies by dropping us off so we would not have to walk all the way from the parking lot to the front door. She was trying to do something nice for us but disregarded our desire. I love her dearly and value her friendship. I am thankful because this experience helped me grow and enhanced awareness of my own actions.

This behavior is typical of society today. We are often busy doing what we want for someone else rather than assessing what might be best for them. As a mother, I spent years making food for my family that I did not wish to eat. This is doing with the other person in mind. There were many other areas of my life where I was not as successful. While reading Jeremiah chapters 42–44 I realized that time and again I disregarded God's desire and instructions. Just like this Ikea story, I asked God for directions and then continued to make my own determination. God told me how he wanted me to choose, and I often neglected his advice and made my own choices—with justification of course. I asked God when I already drew my own conclusion. I also realized I was responding to God with, "I just thought..."

In Jeremiah, God's people pleaded to God for guidance with a promise to fully obey him regardless of what God's call to action was. They pledged that if God would come to their rescue, they would *fully* obey and do as God wanted them to do with their lives. I've had a few of these life situations. I remember being caught deep in sin and begging God to come to my rescue with the promise to be 100 percent committed. There were also the times we experienced financial crisis, physical crisis, or even praying on behalf of a loved one. Unfortunately, after the crisis was averted and life went back to autopilot, my focus was distracted again, and I found myself busy and no longer intently listening to God. God's people in Jeremiah did the same thing. These people of Judah asked God for direction, God gave them the choice to rely on him or self/others, and the people made their own determinations. When crisis was averted, these people continued making a choice to listen to self/others instead of God. They went back to their "normal" and disregarded God's instructions. They stopped listening to God. They did not listen or pay attention, and scripture referred to this as evil actions that God hates. Whether choices come in large decisions or small events, God is not honored or pleased when he comes to the rescue only to later be forgotten.

In my life, I was learning the importance of listening to hear: hearing what someone is communicating and making wise choices, choosing between the "old way" and the "good way," and learning to make *good* choices. Choices that are better for my own self-care and for those around me. Choices that not only please God but brought God glory. I needed to listen to learn and accept what God was speaking to me. I physically needed to listen to my midlife body and accept myself for who I was and where I was on my journey. I needed to love myself and continue to learn. I needed to hold onto what I was learning and continue forward.[1] I needed to keep learning what God wanted me to do by letting the Holy Spirit lead me[2] because true children of God let the Holy Spirit lead them.[3]

Matthew 11:28 shares three action steps that are important to engage simultaneously. This passage of scripture states that we must *come, accept,* and *learn.* Learning is a separate action step that needs application. In this scripture we are encouraged to specifically learn from Christ. We have already talked about the importance of belief and intentionality. I can believe that my children love me, my gal friends value my friendship, or that God has something better for me. The next action step is to *truly* believe it. To activate my belief, accept myself and others for who they are, and then continue to learn from situations and life events. To begin listening to hear God and my inner self, so then I could listen to learn to grow and live a more successful, full life.

Yes, listening to learn is an important action step. The book of Jeremiah shares that for twenty-three years, the prophet Jeremiah shared God's message to the people of Judah. These were God's people, and they needed to stop what they were doing and listen and pay attention to God's specific instructions. These people were going through spiritual motions, worshipping God at the temple and busy doing "good" things, but not listening to God and learning what God desired. God wanted his people to return to him with their whole heart—mind, will, heart, and understanding. Their whole self—all, totality. They needed to learn specifically what God wanted. To be God pleasers, not people pleasers. To learn, a person needs to be ready to hear and obey. Just like we talked about with the levels of listening, we need to be like "good soil." This stage of readiness does not usually come naturally, but takes intention and awareness.

Only when we listen to learn are we able hear what God is saying and lean into life the way that *he* desires.

Chapter Eight

LISTENING TO LEAN IN

How we listen determines what we learn and fuels our drive as we lean into life.

There are differences in how we listen. As a child I remember my mother telling me to do many things like go practice piano, clean my room, or even say I'm sorry when I've wronged a sibling with my actions or words. As a midlife woman, specialists and doctors tell me how to take care of my body by regularly fueling it with whole foods, limiting sugar intake, and eliminate processed foods from my diet. *But*, when someone offers me a cookie or it is a hot summer day and I drive by the ice cream stand, it is often difficult to listen to the wise advice the professional offered. Now, I'm not preaching here that we should never "treat" ourselves. The point is that I seem to only listen to the advice that I prefer to hear. As a wellness coach, people ask my advice on how to lose weight or what healthier decisions they can make. What they generally are asking is assistance for a quick fix and are not intending to stop eating what they desire to eat. A great example can be women and wine. Not being an avid wine drinker, I can't relate, because my vice is water, thankfully. But if someone told me that I couldn't drink water, I wouldn't be able to exist. (Yes, I know I need water to survive.) But I *love* water and every couple hours my body tells me that I need to drink. Here is an example:

A couple days ago was my birthday and my husband took me out for morning fishing. Knowing my water addiction and own body awareness, I filled my favorite water container, that has my grandson's pictures all over it, and packed it for the trip because I didn't want to be without water for the few hours in the boat. Drinking lake water was not an option—yuck. When we got out to the fishing spot at the end of the peninsula where I grew up, near the big buoy, I began to organize myself for fishing. Yes, I must be organized so I'm ready to scoop up a big fish. When I bent down to grab my water container, I noticed that it had spilled out and there was only a trickle left in the bottom. I quickly subsided my panic and had to set my mindset, telling myself to take a sip and it wouldn't be long until I could fill it up again. Life didn't end.

Might sound crazy, but most of us have something that we cannot psychologically live without. Again, I am thankful that my vice is water. For many women, that vice is wine or coffee. Sometimes both. A couple of years ago at a lady's weekend retreat, one I was not speaking at, I got up early in the morning and went to the main reception area. I sat in this big, brown, oversized comfy chair to do morning devotions. As I spent time with God for a couple hours that morning I was amazed and distracted by the dozen or so women who kept walking in looking to see if there was coffee available. Now the event center employees had not gotten up early to start coffee for these ladies and the result was astounding to me. I was amazed by the moans, groans, and looks of disgust, and fright, from these zombie looking ladies as they discovered the empty coffee pots. They seemed unable to survive or even begin their day until they had their hot steaming cup of java.

Wine, I've found, is very similar. Not that a woman can't start her day without it, but wine is a vice that as a coach I am often encouraged to not dictate or limit. Wine is needed to calm a woman and to treat herself after a hard afternoon, day, or week. However, wine and midlife are a difficult pairing. Drinking wine can escalate many midlife challenges, including hot flashes and night sweats. If you are a wine-loving-sister, hold tight, we will dive deeper into this topic in the upcoming guidebook

So, back to my point. We have choices, but even with an open mind and wanting to listen to learn, there are some things that we do not want to follow. How many doctors tell their patients to change their behavior to assist with their diabetes, weight gain, heart issues, etc. only to have the patient leave, engage in the same eating and movement patterns, and return to their next office visit either the same or sicker? Listening is a skill that needs to be developed. I learned that it was important to be aware of my listening style and self-assess before taking positive forward steps.

Looking back, I also found that if I liked something, I was successful at it. I enjoyed sports like soccer, volleyball, and water skiing. I was very successful in those areas. As a student I enjoyed math and gym class, so of course I excelled. Now history on the other hand, was not an interesting subject to me, so I failed to apply myself and did poorly in those classes. The difference was *whether* I applied myself or not.

Listening to lean in to a successful life, to a healthier me took intention along with application. I needed to choose to do what was required whether I preferred it or not. When it comes to choices, my coaching style is not to totally restrict something, because we all have probably experienced that restricting generally involves a relapse or a negative outcome. Instead, replacing and regulating usually increases positive results.

Personally, I was learning I needed to listen with the intention of getting to the finish line. I established why I desired results and wanted to make positive choices to get there, enjoying the journey along the way of course. I needed to be willing to make changes in my life even though these choices might not be easy, exciting, or even enjoyable at times. I knew I wanted what the Bible promised—peace, joy, safety, love, and acceptance. I wanted to feel valued and loved.

Reading Proverbs chapters 3–4, I was intrigued by the question they posed: "What would make my life successful?" Pondering my answer, I came up with a healthy body, a healthy mind, healthy relationships, being respected, being loved, no fear, peace, joyfulness, feeling safe, and feeling protected from the unexpected. My list wasn't money, a big house, or a fancy car. By this point in life, I had learned what matters most was relationships. I enjoy money and nice things, but my end goal is helping others. When I have money,

I *love* to bargain shop so I have more money to cook for others, share with my neighbor, and buy things that my husband would enjoy. So, the instruction in this Proverbs passage was to listen to God's teaching and pay attention—to learn and accept what God says. I needed to both *listen attentively* and *learn to accept* what I was taught to live a long life. So, once I learned to listen, the way I responded and applied myself mattered. I needed to listen with the intention to lean in.

Listening and learning to successfully lean in, I found I needed to *remember* what I was taught[1] and to hold on to it so I could continue to live a successful life. This was a continuous process. Excitedly, with an obedient, open mind, I was discovering God's true purpose for my life. What I began discovering was there were things I have always wanted in my life, things I felt were impossible, things that I truly enjoyed doing, and things at which I was very good. Now I needed to figure out how these lined up with God's intended plan for my life and what God was specifically calling me to do. I *wanted* to *listen*, *wanted* to *learn*, and was ready to *lean in* regardless of what was asked of me.

There is a song called "Oceans" with the call to let the Holy Spirit "lead me where my trust is without borders, let me walk upon the water, wherever God may call me. Take me deeper where my feet will never wander, where my faith will be made stronger in the presence of my Savior."[2] I did not realize how my walk was going to be tested with this heart's desire. I was learning from scripture there was *a plan, a purpose, a partner, a power,* and *a promise* from God specifically with my life.[3]

There is a specific plan for your life as well.

God's *plan* in Romans 8:28–39 was destined even before I was born. His plan for me is to belong to him. I am called and chosen to love God. To be his people. My *purpose* is to be like his son, Jesus Christ who walked the earth so many years ago to show me how to live a perfect life. Regardless of my circumstances, God's call is to belong and be today whom he created me to be. I am made right with God, so that he may be glorified.

My *partner* is the Holy spirit, which is the first part of God's promise. The Holy Spirit came to live within me and help me when I asked Jesus to forgive my sins. The Holy Spirit empowers me to make good decisions and choices that please God.

My *power* is the truth that if God is for me, who can be against me? *No one.* With God's power working in me, I can do much, much more than I could ever ask or imagine.[4]

The *promise* is full of victories through God who showed me his love by offering relationship with him through Jesus. *Nothing* can or will separate me from his love. As I persevere in doing the will of God, I receive the benefits he promised.

In light of his promise, power, and partnership, my purpose is to daily *let* the Holy Spirit lead me. The Holy Spirit will do the same in you. You have different talents, and your talents are just as important as my talents. The key to spiritual health is to listen to *hear*, listen to *learn*, and listen to *lean* into what or who God is calling us be today. We are not created to just exist and do good things we enjoy. We have talents for a greater purpose.

Intentionally activating our listening activates our living.

SECTION 4

Active Living

ACTIVE LIVING

Active living involves continuing.

A ctive living is to take what is working—what is learned, active belief, and active listening—and continue with it.

The energizer bunny needed batteries to activate it and then needed these same batteries to help it continue forward in action. When this bunny's batteries were depleted, it stopped movement. Battery power was needed for the bunny to continue.

Likewise, intentionality and specific action are needed to help us activate our daily lives. Galatians chapter 3 shares that when we receive the Holy Spirit by hearing and believe Jesus's full story, our life in Christ with the help of the Holy Spirit begins. We are to continue hearing, believing, and receiving not with our own power but by using the Holy Spirit's energizing power. That is the journey. To know our identity, value, purpose, and worth, to keep focus, and then continue. Continuing with confidence to find a better life balance that leads to experiencing Whole-Self Health.

Chapter Nine
CONTINUE WITH CONFIDENCE

Have you ventured outside your comfort zone with confidence before?

A few years ago, my mother, sister, and I took a trip to NYC, and we decided to attend a viewing of a morning talk show called, *Kelly and Ryan*. We had our tickets and arrived at the break of dawn, waiting in a long line that curved around the block of tall skyscrapers. When we finally got inside to a seat in the back row, near where the celebrities and guests entered, there was a request for volunteers. Before I knew what came over me, my hand went up and moments later I was in front of the few hundred audience members participating in a dance-off contest. As I looked to my right and left, there were other contestants gyrating their hips, and I began to panic realizing what I had gotten myself into. Clear thinking ensued and I decided that I did not want to win this competition and be on national television demonstrating my newfound confidence. I tried to act engaged in what appeared to be entertainment at the expense of audience members and hastily made my way to my back corner seat, mortified and laughing at myself.

My striving to be more confident in who I was and stepping out by not allowing fear to control my mind, thoughts, actions, and intentions got me into an unexpected predicament. Lower levels of estrogen are bitter sweet. Confidence can come easy, and at the same time be a bit "out-of-control." Lower estrogen production from a women's ovaries, Dr. Henry Hess writes in his book *The Perfect Menopause*, is a described as a hallmark of menopause. The decrease of estrogen brings an increase of other body chemicals, something we will dive into deeper with my next book. In meno, our female bodies are adapting. Often clearer thinking is joined by sporadic behaviors and attitudes that can be mirrored to the beginning of our fertile cycle—puberty. It was this experience that taught me I needed to be mindful of when and how I choose to demonstrate my determination. This great learning experience was a steppingstone. My confidence needed to be clear-cut, certain, and controlled.

Not only in midlife, but with age comes an increased level of self-efficacy. I mentioned earlier that I was preparing for a women's workshop this past month, where I was asked to speak on mental health and the mind. Excited to speak at this state workshop, I learned even more about mental health and the aging mind. One of my "Eight Steps to Improve Your Aging Mind" is to engage in positive self-talk with confidence. While learning that aging adults experience an increase in self-efficacy, my behavior the couple years prior in the dance-off in front of a studio audience was better explained. Self-efficacy is a person's belief in his or her ability to succeed in a particular situation. This confidence and belief in oneself are attributes to be celebrated. Celebrated, but controlled.

I was learning how to continue.
I needed to progress, to advance.

My life's aim has not changed since that day in tenth grade when God got my attention. Back in 1983, I began to serve God in many capacities. At church I worked with children in the nursery, and teen ministry, taught Sunday school, sang in choir, and continued performing solos. At private school I joined a girl's traveling singing group and went on a mission trip asking God to use me to share and invite others into his family of believers. I tried being intentional with my life, with a goal of pleasing God. I thought I had a boring testimony and a very healthy spiritual life aside from a couple of speed bumps in the road or short detours. But the busyness of life continued creeping in and distracting me. I started my day with good intentions, but before I knew it my mind was elsewhere with other things becoming a larger priority than thinking about God.

For many years, my spouse and boys were a higher priority than God in my life. I felt God would understand because I honored God by being a good wife and mother. My service to God was taking care of my family. There were some very rocky years and looking back I know now God wanted to be first priority. Life would have been quite different if I had continued in the way God asked me.

Continuing was challenging.

Have you had seasons in your life where God was calling you to draw closer to him, but you were too busy to spend time reading his word? I remember those years wondering "when?" My schedule was so packed, I couldn't even imagine juggling one more thing. My justification was that God knew my heart, loved me, and would understand. It was busyness and good intentions that were my struggle in continuing. I proceeded, turned on autopilot for daily living, and God was put by the wayside. Many situations and crisis that came my way should have been a reminder or triggered my awareness I was not living as close to God as I should have been. There were many predicaments where I stopped and cried out to God. It was almost like I would had to look for him to engage with him. "Help me, Jesus, where are you?" I knew God was always close by and would help me in time of need, but my reaction was to look for him only when I needed him instead of walking by his side already holding his hand when dilemmas arose. I was learning that God wanted more. God wanted a higher level of intimacy. To successfully continue, my aim needed to be focused on *thinking* about what God wants; *knowing* my value, purpose, and calling; *doing* what God requires; and *being* who God wants me to be.

THINKING

Have you ever heard the adage, "Your thoughts rule your life?" My master's in human services and coaching required reading countless books on positive thinking. Over and over, I learned our mindset could affect us positively or negatively—personally, professionally, spiritually, relationally, and physically. My continued education on women in midlife furthered this need to engage in positive self-talk. Even today, I find enjoyment in teaching women how to spin midlife stigmas into esteem. We must believe the truths and call out the lies. Once we call out these lies, we need to give action to our desires.

In my spiritual life, I needed to call out the lies and do "good things" differently than I had been doing. Reading Romans chapters 7–8, I am encouraged to *think* about what God wants. I am reminded that God determines (sets) my value and worth. I need to want to do "good things" and choose the "good way." To experience true life and be a true child of God, as Paul promised in Romans, I needed to distinguish between what I wanted and what God wanted. Following my selfish motivations would result in death—death of relationships, death of self-worth, struggle with providence, and an overall harder life experience because I was being disobedient to God. Instead, if I would engage in doing what God wanted by allowing the Holy Spirit to lead me, following the spirit would result in fullness of life and peace. Old self is ruled by ideas that are opposed to God, and the new self is ruled by Christ through the Holy Spirit. I needed to set my mind on things that were good, pleasing, acceptable, and perfect.[1] Keeping my thoughts focused would give me the confidence to remember and know God more intimately.

KNOWING

Confidence in knowing is important. Let's use some simple examples to make this point because there are some things that we know and some things we *know*. Have you had that discussion with a spouse, family member, child, or friend? A conversation recalling a situation that happened or a memory from the past? Some memories are recalled with an approximate remembrance and there are other memories that are recalled with confidence. I know what was said, what I said, what happened, and remember like yesterday the results. I *know* that I *know*. This is what I would like to frame as "knowing with confidence."

Now let's talk about continuing with confidence. Scripture has been teaching me that I can *know* my value, worth, purpose, and calling. My calling is to continue discovering what God wants me to do for him every day instead of what others determine I should be or do. I remember the ah-ha moment reading the passage found in Romans chapter 7 backed up against Romans chapter 8. Romans chapter 7 describes our daily challenges, how I continue to do the things I don't want to do instead of doing the things that I should do. The struggle of not doing the good things I want to do, but instead, doing the things I don't want to do. My whole life I lived in this crazy cycle. My wants, needs, and desires constantly caught up in busyness and distractions around me. My mind and body often being on two different paths. My old self desiring to be new but continuing to go off on a detour in the wrong direction. The solution is found in Romans chapter 8: the new self engaging with the power of the Holy Spirit living within—the key, the secret, the answer. Being made new and having the help of the Holy Spirit to continue in my new self, I was reminded to allow my thinking to be controlled by the Holy Spirit. I felt like a superhero. I had supernatural power and I should be confident and *know* in whom I believe and be faithful to continue. This mindset and confidence activates my doing.

DOING

We talked about the book of Jeremiah earlier. God was urging his people to do what *he* specifically was asking them, instead of what they wanted to do *for* him. God wanted them to return with their whole hearts—mind, will, and understanding. God duplicated this message in Isaiah when he urged his people to stop trying and start doing. I surfed the words "trying versus doing" and I came up with this enlightenment.

> "*Trying* is not the same as *doing*. You
> either *do* something or you don't.
> When we say we are *trying*,
> we don't have to *do* anything.
> It only provides us with an excuse
> or why we couldn't accomplish
> the outcome we desired."[2]

Wow! I spent my life *trying* to honor God. Trying gave me excuses why I didn't end up with results that I wanted. Now that I confidently know whom I am, I am committed to do what I know needs to be done. By hearing, believing, and being intentional, I make better choices to live wisely day-to-day and start being who I was called to be.

BEING

My Christian walk has been like a winding road and often very confusing. As I shared, being told how to act and behave and discovering that my instruction quite often did not match up to what I was learning in God's word gave me the gumption to begin digging into the Bible for myself to seek out the truths and replace the lies. Even today sitting in a teaching session or sermon I hear some of the old Christian sayings that send me into a frenzy seeking to read the teaching lesson in context with what God's word directly says to me. I sit there physically crossing out the lies on paper and writing out the truths to reprogram my mind and thoughts. I am focused. I want to learn to become who God wants me to be by listening, thinking, and doing what God wants.

God's word is not confusing. My job is to be attentive and ready because God might call me to do the unexpected. God wants more for me. With the Holy Spirit living within me, God can do much more that I could ever ask or begin to imagine.[3]

We do not know what tomorrow brings, so today I need to choose the good way. Be obedient. Be ready. Life is not promised to be easy, but we are encouraged to be careful how we live every day. We are to be careful to make wise choices and use every chance for doing good things while continuing to learn what God wants us to do. I am on a journey of purpose, meaning, hope, strength, and confidence. I *know* that I *know*, and my mindset is on a constant re-set. Now I needed to balance it!

Chapter Ten

CONTINUE WITH BALANCE

Balance can be challenging during our bookend years *(beginning and end of life)*. A baby needs to learn to balance their body as they begin learning to walk and an aging adult learns that their equilibrium changes as the years pass. Maintaining balance in our midlife is often a challenge mentally, physically, and relationally. I was out of town working remotely in Massachusetts a couple months ago when my husband and I decided to take an adventurous walk during lunch. We both love being outdoor active adventurers, so we decided to walk up the stream and see if there was a waterfall to be discovered. As we walked, we noticed there were trees that had fallen across the stream and my husband decided to cross the stream using one of these natural bridges. Not as daring as he,

I decided to walk a little farther to cross using a larger surface area. As I stepped out onto the log, I discovered that my balance is not what it used to be, and not what I anticipated it would be. Unsure of myself I continued to put one foot in front of the other, focusing on the other side. My intention was to get to the other bank to continue the adventure walk with my spouse. As I got about a third of the way across, panic set in and I knew it was unsafe for me to continue. Looking behind me and in front of me, I was hesitant to move but found that standing still posed an even larger threat. As my body started to teeter, I compensated by taking small steps backward while praying I could keep my balance until I safely returned to the bank.

What an eye-opening experience for me.

I am learning as I grow older and wiser, that there may be some things that I "can" do, but I need to assess if these are things that I "should "do. I learned some important lessons that day. I learned my physical balance has new limitations. Also, moving forward was easier than moving backward, but standing still was not an option. Jack Travis' Illness-Wellness Continuation Theory states, if we are not going one direction, we are going another. We are either making choices that lead us to wellness or choices that lead us to sickness. Albert Einstein had a similar thought, that to keep our balance riding a bicycle, one needs to keep moving. To keep balance, the body needs movement, not stagnation.

The fear that crept into my outdoor adventure that day may have subsided if I'd just remained focused on the goal of getting to the other side, but another option was to listen to my body, consider my limitations, and make wiser choices. I made a *good choice* and reconnected with my husband a few yards downstream. Balance needs movement and movement is needed to continue.

FINDING A BETTER BALANCE

As a life balance professional speaker, I get the opportunity to teach people through workshops, seminars, and keynote presentations. One presentation is called, "How to Create a Balanced Life: Nine Tips to Feel Calm and Grounded." I deliver other messages that describe strategies to engage in better balance and share that balance takes thought, work, and intention. We will dive in deeper into this topic with the upcoming guidebook.

To be balanced it is important to have a handle on various elements of your life so that your mind and heart are not pulled too far in any direction. Balance assists in experiencing clearer thinking, increased energy, motivation, and finding time to make better choices regardless of circumstances. On my adventure walk that beautiful day in the woods, I needed to handle my crisis, re-assess what my mind told me I could do, and get a handle on my physical balance. The more I study, the more I learn how important balance is.

When someone's life is out of balance it generally means that they are being pulled in two or more directions. Can you relate with this? Every day I scuffle with busyness and distractions to find a better personal life balance. I've learned that finding balance starts internally. I need to find my own internal balance before introducing external elements. As I balance my mind, body, and spirit (relationship with God and others), I can better stabilize my external areas—home, family, work, friends. This book about my journey has been exactly this. When I began focusing on my personal health, making healthier choices using the help of the Holy Spirit and a coach, I more frequently choose the *good way*. My mind and heart are better focused together, and I experience a better life balance. Knowing, Doing, Remembering, and Continuing with confidence I am less distracted and able to better fixate on listening to God. My self-awareness and others-awareness is increased, and forward motion occurs.

We've talked about how God's people did not listen to him. Instead they did what they desired and ignored God. God wanted his people to be his people in action and he wanted to be their God in return. But their lack of listening, paying attention, and self-focus perturbed God as he told them they were moving backward not forward.[1] My life has been muddled with forward and backward momentum physically, spiritually, and mentally. I was learning that better balance was experienced with forward movement. There are many books in the Bible, as I've shared in this book, that talk about how God's people did what *they* wanted to do. This applies to me today, and if I'm not mindful I can find myself quickly back in this very place. As I shared with you, I spent many years busy in ministry and service doing *for* God. When I do *for* God, I am moving backward, but if I do *with* God using the help of the Holy Spirit so God can be seen and glorified, I am engaging in a positive, full, joy-filled, peace-filled, successful life of forward momentum, striving for "Whole-Self Health."

Chapter Eleven
WHOLE-SELF HEALTH

What is whole-self health?

Whole-self health means finding balance in all areas of life—mentally, physically, and spiritually.

Each one of these areas is important, and these independent areas affect each other.

If you have physical ailments, it can affect your mindset and how you relate with others. Women in midlife often have night sweats or hot flashes that can cause lack of sleep (physical) and irritability dealing with daily nonsense (mental and/or spiritual/relational). Each of these areas are connected and affect each other. The goal is to find an individualized balance. In my life, I have learned the importance of balancing my mindset, sleep, movement, water intake, and relationships with God, spouse, kids, family, co-workers, and friends. By focusing on my internal before my external, I listen to my body and self-talk while listening, learning, and leaning in to God's word that tells me God wants my Whole Being.[1] God wants my whole self (mind, body, spirit) to live blameless.[2] My whole self in the Greek translation is *holoteleis*[3] which means "complete, perfect." God was stating that he wanted my whole self, my entire self, my complete and perfect self in its entirety. God wants my spirit (pneuma), my soul (psyche), and my physical body (soma), to live pure and without blame—belonging only to him, especially in this unpredictable, overwhelming world in which we live. Finding true balance is hard to obtain or experience without the help of God through the Holy Spirit.

THE HOW TO

You cannot imagine my excitement while reading the book of Proverbs when I stumbled on the fourth chapter. Always wanting and striving for balance, the "how-to" was often unclear. Have you ever wanted something but were not sure how to get it? Now this could be as simple as I would like to buy that black dress or strapless shoes but not sure how to come up with the money to pay for them, or I want to lose weight and not find it again but am not sure how to successfully accomplish that. I remember the years that I wanted intimate relationships but was unsuccessful and would have liked a "how-to" manual.

Reading Proverbs 4:2–27, I was elated to read that there were keys to life for those who find them. These keys, God shared, bring health to the whole body. God was sharing guidance to finding whole-self health. My years of searching for answers were found here in this short passage. Some seasons in life I had a healthy body, other seasons I had healthy relationships, and on the rare occasion my mindset had a good run. But the balance of all three of these areas have *always* been a struggle. I was not looking for perfection, just a better balance. I wanted to feel whole, healthy, happy, and content. So, what were these keys that God was sharing that brought health to the whole body? There were four instructions, and it was exciting that I had already begun working on them.

First, I was to be careful of my thoughts because my thoughts rule my life. Secondly, I was encouraged to use my mouth and words to always be truthful. Third, I was to keep my focus on what is right and look straight ahead at what is good. Interesting how these first three involve the head—brain, mouth, and eyes. Lastly, I was commanded to be careful with my actions and to always do what is right—to keep on the road of goodness and stay away from evil paths. This was exactly what God was teaching me on my journey.

This book duplicates those instructions. Yes, I needed to mind my mindset and my mouth. I need to speak positive truths to myself and others. I was also learning that I needed to put proper fuel into my mouth. I needed to eat nutrients that fueled and healed my body. I have a vintage plaque in my kitchen that reads, "Lord, fill my mouth with worthwhile stuff and nudge me when I said enough." As a typical middle child, I find my mouth still needs to be properly guarded and maintained. As a wellness coach, I know I need to be mindful and fuel my body with nutrients that are beneficial.

The last instruction was to be careful with what I do and to *always* do what is right to keep on the road of goodness and away from evil paths. Yes, I needed to pause when choices needed to be made and choose between the old way and the good way. I needed to choose the good way and keep focused ahead of me. I needed to take one step at a time. I needed to celebrate each step. I needed to remember that small steps in the right direction *are* important.[4] I needed to pay attention to these words, listen closely, and not forget them. I needed to be mindful of these words and keep them always in mind. These words *are* key to life and will bring health to the *whole body*, to those who find them. I wanted to be one who found these words. I wanted to continue. I wanted to embrace these words, remember, and continue.

Deuteronomy 4:29 says, "God wants us to look for him with our whole hearts, our whole being, so that we can find him." The results are life altering. The outcome is the promise of experiencing a full life. Jesus shared the secret to life in Luke 10:27–28. He shared that the actions that offer life, eternal life, is to "Love the Lord your God with *all* your heart, *all* your soul, *all* your strength, and *all* your mind." Also, "Love your neighbor as yourself." By engaging my whole self, I was finally experiencing full life, satisfaction, success, and a better life balance.

FINAL WORDS

Today, I am still a work-in-progress. How I choose to start and live each day has changed. My life is a continual journey, and my aim, focus, and actions continue to progress. I am on an adventure to daily spend time reading God's word to continue believing, listening, doing, and being who God wants me to be. I am going to continue leaning into life with my whole heart. When I find that I venture off path, I am going to return quickly and continue forward. God has a special plan for my life. God has placed a call on my life to encourage women—embolden *all* women—whether they know Jesus or not. My call is to journey with women and inspire them to imagine or re-imagine their potential, so they will believe in themselves, so we can together make a difference in this world. We are better together. This is my story, my journey, and I have never been happier or experienced peace like I do today. I would not change anything because my experiences have made me into the woman I am. I am confident, courageous, and don't expect life to be easy.

By sharing my story, my aim is to allow my past to be the hope for your future. My heart breaks seeing women so tired, burned out, and hopeless, with little self-care or needed support which impacts their family, relationships, health, vitality, and life. I am committed to helping women reach their potential through knowing, being, and doing together. Women *are* powerful and need to claim the power they already have inside themselves. I am a women's ally through midlife transition and change. Currently dealing with my second round of meno and battling the midlife middle *again* head-on, my hardship incites me to support women side-by-side. Women in midlife and beyond have so many different challenges, which is why I began a Midlife Mutiny. Midlife prompts social, mental, chemical, and physical changes and there is still limited information and few non-pharmaceutical solutions. All women need a relatable and reliable ally. I step up to that challenge.

FINAL WORDS

As I broke through the crisis, conflicts, and stigmas associated with midlife and menopause, I now wish to embolden you to do the same.

Stay tuned for the next book, which is a guidebook to whole-self health. We are all unique and I am very excited to share strategies in all areas, uncover stigmas, and address the midlife symptoms so you too can become a confident, worthy, and hope-filled woman.

Until then, speak kindly to yourself, you are worth it!

YOU CAN HELP

THANK YOU FOR READING MY BOOK!

I appreciate all your feedback and would love to hear what you have to say, because your input helps to improve the next version of this book as well as my future books.
Every review matters *a lot!*

So please head over to Amazon or wherever you purchased this book and leave me an honest review.

Thank you so much!
Ala Ladd

ACKNOWLEDGMENTS

I would like to thank my family and friends who have taken the time to pour into my life over the years. Extended thanks to my coaches and co-writers at Self-Publishing School. Every great coach needs to utilize the assistance of a coach to persevere in their craft.

I'm looking forward to sharing my next guidebook, followed by the expert compilation, and especially assisting women by helping them to step out and share their own stories with the world.

ABOUT THE AUTHOR

Ala began her journey in business and fitness when graduating with an associate degree from Palm Beach Atlantic College, FL in 1990. Decades later she found that serving the roles of wife, mother, and corporate manager, she needed to find herself an ally to assist in her journey back to improved health and wellness. Finding success with a coach, her life was re-directed to help others get control over their health. Learning that optimal health requires more than diet and exercise, Ala branded "Help Getting Healthy," became a credentialed Health Coach, Corporate Wellness Coach, Health & Wellness Coach, Lifestyle Fitness Coach, Professional Speaker, and completed a master's in Human Services/Coaching at Liberty University.

Ala lives in upstate NY, is a woman of faith, and her key audience is professional women in their midlife and beyond. Why? Because midlife prompts social, mental, chemical, and physical changes which require the need for women to reexamine themselves. Her pursuit is to help empower women in their mid-life to reach their full potential by using relationship-based, client-centered, and goal-driven approaches.

As a professional Lifestyle Balance ally, Ala co-creates alliances and commits through speaking, writing, coaching, seminars, retreats, and wellness workshops to take the journey with women to help them find their own individual balance in life mentally, physically, and spiritually .

REFERENCES

BibleHub.com. (n.d.). Retrieved from http:/www.thebiblehub.com

Foster, R. J. (2018). *Celebration of Discipline: The Path to Spiritual Growth*. New York: Harper Collins.

Hess, Henry M. Dr, M.D., P. D. (2008). *The Perfect Menopause: 7 Steps to the Best Time of Your Life*. Rochester: Westfall Park Publishing Group.

Menopause. (n.d.). Retrieved from http:/www.cdc.gov

Moore, B. (2007). *Jesus: 90 Days with The One and Only*. Nashville: B&H Press.

Myers, J. R. (2003). *The Search to Belong: Rethinking Intimacy, Community, and Small Groups*. Grand Rapids: Zondervan.

REFERENCES

Peterson, J. C. (2007). *Why Don't We Listen Better?* Peterson Publications.

The North American Menopause Society. (n.d.). Retrieved from http:/www.menopause.org

Thesaurus. (n.d.). Retrieved from http:/www.thesaurus.com

Tips to Help You Stay Young. (n.d.). Retrieved from http:/www.realbuzz.com*Trying-vs-Doing. (n.d.). Retrieved from https://deepstash.com/idea/26351/trying-vs-doing*

Travis, J. (2004). *The Wellness Workbook: How to Achieve Enduring Health and Vitality.* Berkeley: Ten Speed Press.

Unless otherwise noted, Scripture is taken from the New Century Version (NCV), copyright © 2005 by Thomas Nelson, Inc. All rights reserved.

SPEAKING TOPICS

- **Balancing Your Mental Health:** 8 Steps to Improve the Maturing Mind
- **5 Ways to Improve Work Productivity**
- **Finding Contentment in a Crisis**
- **How 2 Find Time in Your Busy Schedule:** *Looking beyond your circumstances to find meaning, purpose, hope through balance.*
- **Finding Balance Through the Busy**
- **I'll Sleep When I'm Dead** *or* **The Skinny on Sleep** *(Title depends on age demographic.)*
- **10 Things to Look Forward to in Midlife**
- **More than Managing Your Menopause:** *6 Steps to Help Women through Mid-Life's Transitions and Change*
- **Clean Eating 101**

SPEAKING TOPICS

- **How to Guarantee a Successful Life:** *Listen, Learn, Lean In*
- **Thriving Through the Hustle**
- **Living Well... What Pop Culture Does Not Want You to Know!**

More wellness and faith-based topics available on request

END NOTES

THE BEGINNING

1. Romans 10:14
2. Romans 10:11

1. BALANCING BUMMERS

1. Romans 3-4
2. Romans 4
3. Ephesians 4:22-24; 2 Corinthians 5:17

2. CONTINUING CONCERNS

1. Romans 7:15-20
2. 1 Thessalonians 5:23; Proverbs 4:20-27; James 4:7-10; Psalms 34; Deuteronomy 30
3. Philippians 1:6

ACTIVE BELIEF

1. https://www.thesaurus.com/browse/inactive
2. https://www.thesaurus.com/browse/active

3. RE-AWAKENING

1. John 14:6
2. John 14:1
3. https://www.thesaurus.com/browse/aspire
4. 1 Thessalonians 5
5. 1 Peter 2:17
6. 1 Peter 4:1
7. Isaiah 53:10
8. Isaiah 64:4-5
9. Isaiah 61:9; 66:19

4. INTENTIONALITY

1. https://www.dictionary.com/browse/intention
2. 2 Corinthian 5:17

5. BECOMING

1. 1 Peter 1:13; Philippians 4:8; Romans 12:2; Colossians 3:2; Romans 8:5-7
2. https://positivepsychology.com/self-efficacy/
3. Jeremiah 6:16
4. Ephesians 5

6. LISTENING TO HEAR

1. https://www.dictionary.com/browse/parable
2. Isaiah 6:9-10
3. Mark 4:10
4. Mark 4:9

END NOTES

7. LISTENING TO LEARN

1. Proverbs 4:13
2. Ephesians 5:17-18
3. Romans 8:4-8,14

8. LISTENING TO LEAN IN

1. Proverbs 4:2
2. https://www.google.com/search?client=safari&rls=en&q=hillsong+oceans&ie=UTF-8&oe=UTF-8
3. Romans 8:28-39
4. Ephesians 3:20

9. CONTINUE WITH CONFIDENCE

1. Philippians 4:8
2. https://deepstash.com/idea/26351/trying-vs-doing
3. Ephesians 3:20

10. CONTINUE WITH BALANCE

1. Jeremiah 7:21-26

11. WHOLE-SELF HEALTH

1. Psalms 34:2
2. 1 Thessalonians 5:23
3. https://biblehub.com/text/1_thessalonians/5-23.htm
4. Zechariah 4:10

Made in the USA
Middletown, DE
24 November 2021